*Praise for Montana 1948*

'Meditative, rich, and written close to the bone, *Montana 1948* is a beautiful novel about the meaning of place and evolution of courage. It is wonderful book'

LOUISE ERDRICH

'A literary page-turner, morally complex and satisfying in its careful accumulation of detail and in its use of landscape to reveal character'

KIRKUS REVIEWS

'Watson indelibly portrays the moral dilemma of a family torn between justice and loyalty; by implication, he also illuminates some dark corners of our national history'

PUBLISHER'S WEEKLY

'A simple but powerful tale . . . Watson is to be congratulated for the honesty of his writing and the purity of his prose'

LIBRARY JOURNAL

'The relationship of landscape to personality is a familiar theme, especially in western literature, but it may never have been explored with as much sensitivity and as fine an eye for detail as Watson manages in this stunning coming-of-age novel . . . The unspoken life of any small town, especially a small, hardscrabble western town, contains a motherlode of raw emotion, morally ambiguous and potentially devastating. Watson mines that vein with unflinching honesty and complete respect, both for the dignity of the people and the implacability of the landscape'

BOOKLIST

'As universal in its themes as it is original in its particularities, *Montana 1948* is a significant and elegant addition to the fiction of the American West'

WASHINGTON POST

'The style is as thin, clear and crisp as a North Dakota wind. It mirrors the landscape of his story; it is appropriate to the plain-spoken characters he creates'

LOS ANGELES TIMES BOOK REVIEW

Also by Larry Watson

*In a Dark Time*

*Leaving Dakota*

# *Montana 1948*

## A Novel

## LARRY WATSON

**MACMILLAN**

First published 1993 by Milkweed Editions, Minneapolis

First published in Great Britain 1995 by Macmillan London
an imprint of Macmillan General Books
Cavaye Place London SW10 9PG
and Basingstoke

Associated companies throughout the world

ISBN 0 333 62820 9

Additional support has been provided by the Elmer and Eleanor Andersen
Foundation; Dayton Hudson Foundation for Dayton's and Target Stores;
First Bank System Foundation; General Mills Foundation; Honeywell
Foundation; Jerome Foundation; The McKnight Foundation; Andrew W.
Mellon Foundation; Minnesota State Arts Board through an appropriation by
the Minnesota State Legislature; Literature and Challenge Programs of the
National Endowment for the Arts, Northwest Area Foundation; I. A.
O'Shaughnessy Foundation; Piper Jaffray Companies, Inc.; John and Beverly
Rollwagen Fund; Surdna Foundation; Lila Wallace-Reader's Digest Literary
Publishers Marketing Development Program, funded through a grant to the
Council of Literary Magazines and Small Presses; and generous individuals.

1 3 5 7 9 8 6 4 2

A CIP catalogue record for this book is available from
the British Library.

Printed and bound in Great Britain by
Mackays of Chatham plc, Chatham, Kent

*For Susan*

*Montana 1948*

# Prologue

✿ ✿ ✿

Fʀᴏᴍ the summer of my twelfth year I carry a series of images more vivid and lasting than any others of my boyhood and indelible beyond all attempts the years make to erase or fade them. . . .

*A young Sioux woman lies on a bed in our house. She is feverish, delirious, and coughing so hard I am afraid she will die.*

*My father kneels on the kitchen floor, begging my mother to help him. It's a summer night and the room is brightly lit. Insects cluster around the light fixtures, and the pleading quality in my father's voice reminds me of those insects—high-pitched, insistent, frantic. It is a sound I have never heard coming from him.*

*My mother stands in our kitchen on a hot, windy day. The windows are open, and Mother's lace curtains blow into the room. Mother holds my father's Ithaca twelve-gauge shotgun, and since she is a small, slender woman, she has trouble finding the balance point of its heavy length. Nevertheless, she has watched my father and other men often enough to know where the shells go, and she loads them until the gun will hold no more. Loading the gun is the difficult part. Once the shells are in, any fool can figure out how to fire it. Which she intends to do.*

There are others—the sound of breaking glass, the odor of rotting vegetables. . . . I offer these images in the order in

11

which they occurred, yet the events that produced these sights and sounds are so rapid and tumbled together that any chronological sequence seems wrong. Imagine instead a movie screen divided into boxes and panels, each with its own scene, so that one moment can occur simultaneously with another, so no action has to fly off in time, so nothing happens before or after, only during. That's the way these images coexist in my memory, like the Sioux picture calendars in which the whole year's events are painted on the same buffalo hide, or like a tapestry with every scene woven into the same cloth, every moment on the same flat plane, the summer of 1948. . . .

Forty years ago. Two months ago my mother died. She made, as the expression goes, a good death. She came inside the house from working in her garden, and a heart attack, as sudden as a sneeze, felled her in the kitchen. My father's death, ten years earlier, was less merciful. Cancer hollowed him out over the years until he could not stand up to a stiff wind. And Marie Little Soldier? Her fate contains too much of the story for me to give away.

A story that is now only mine to tell. I may not be the only witness left—there might still be someone in that small Montana town who remembers those events as well as I, but no one knew all three of these people better.

And no one loved them more.

# One

❀ ❀ ❀

I N 1948 my father was serving his second term as sheriff of Mercer County, Montana. We lived in Bentrock, the county seat and the only town of any size in the region. In 1948 its population was less than two thousand people.

Mercer County is in the far northeast corner of Montana, and Bentrock is barely inside the state's borders. Canada is only twelve miles away (though the nearest border crossing is thirty miles to the west), and North Dakota ten miles. Then, as now, Mercer County was both farm and ranch country, but with only a few exceptions, neither farms nor ranches were large or prosperous. On the western edge of the county and extending into two other counties was the Fort Warren Indian Reservation, the rockiest, sandiest, least arable parcel of land in the region. In 1948 its roads were unpaved, and many of its shacks looked as though they would barely hold back a breeze.

But all of northeastern Montana is hard country—the land is dry and sparse and the wind never stops blowing. The heat and thunderstorms in summer can be brutal, and the winters are legendary for the fierceness of their blizzards and the depths to which temperatures drop. (In one year we reached 106 degrees in July and 40 below in January.) For those of you who automatically think of Montana and snow-capped mountains in the same synapse, let me disabuse you. Mercer County is plains, flat as a tabletop on its western edge and riven with gullies, ravines, and low rocky hills to the east because of the work the Knife River has done over the centuries. The only trees that grow in that part of the country, aside from a few cottonwoods along the riverbank, have been planted by farmers and town dwellers. And they haven't planted many. If the land had its way, nothing would grow taller than sagebrush and buffalo grass.

The harshness of the land and the flattening effect of wind and endless sky probably accounted for the relative tranquility of Mercer County. Life was simply too hard, and so much of your attention and energy went into keeping not only yourself but also your family, your crops, and your cattle alive, that nothing was left over for raising hell or making trouble.

And 1948 still felt like a new, blessedly peaceful era. The exuberance of the war's end had faded but the relief had not. The mundane, workaday world was a gift that had not outworn its shine. Many of the men in Mercer County had spent the preceding years in combat. (But not my father; he was 4-F. When he was sixteen a horse kicked him, breaking his leg so severely that he walked with a permanent limp, and eventually a cane, his right leg V-ed in, his right knee perpetually pointing to the left.) When these men came back from war they wanted nothing more than to work their farms and ranches and to live quietly with their families. The county even had fewer hunters after the war than before.

All of which made my father's job a relatively easy one.

Oh, he arrested the usual weekly drunks, mediated an occasional dispute about fence lines or stray cattle, calmed a few domestic disturbances, and warned the town's teenagers about getting rowdy in Wood's Cafe, but by and large being sheriff of Mercer County did not require great strength or courage. The ability to drive the county's rural roads, often drifted over in the winter or washed out in the summer, was a much more necessary skill than being good with your fists or a gun. One of my father's regular duties was chaperoning Saturday night dances in the county, but the fact that he often took along my mother (and sometimes me) shows how quiet those affairs—and his job—usually were.

And that disappointed me at the time. As long as my father was going to be a sheriff, a position with so much potential for excitement, danger, and bravery, why couldn't some of that promise be fulfilled? No matter how many wheat fields or cow pastures surrounded us, we were still Montanans, yet my father didn't even look like a western sheriff. He wore a shirt and tie, as many of the men in town did, but at least they wore boots and Stetsons; my father wore brogans and a fedora. He had a gun but he never carried it, on duty or off. I knew because I checked, time and time again. When he left the house I ran to his dresser and the top drawer on the right side. And there it was, there it always was. Just as well. As far as I was concerned it was the wrong kind of gun for a sheriff. He should have had a nickel-plated Western Colt .45, something with some history and heft. Instead, my father had a small .32 automatic, Italian-made and no bigger than your palm. My father didn't buy such a sorry gun; he confiscated it from a drunken transient in one of his first arrests. My father kept the gun but in fair exchange bought the man a bus ticket to Billings, where he had family.

The gun was scratched and nicked and had a faint blush of rust along the barrel. The original grips were gone and had been replaced by two cut-to-fit rectangles of Masonite. Every time I came across the gun it was unloaded, its clip full of the short, fat .32 cartridges lying nearby in the same drawer. The pistol slopped about in a thick, stiff leather strap-and-snap holster meant for a larger gun and a revolver at that. Since it looked more like a toy than the western-style cap guns that had been my toys, I wasn't even tempted to take my father's gun out for play, though I had the feeling I could have kept it for weeks and my father wouldn't have missed it.

You're wondering if perhaps my father kept his official side arm in his county jail office. If he did, I never saw it there, and I wandered in and out of that jail office as often as I did the rooms of our home. I saw the rack of rifles and shotguns in their locked case (and two sets of handcuffs looped and dangling from the barrel of a Winchester 94) but no pistols.

We lived, you see, in a white two-story frame house right across the street from the courthouse, and the jail and my father's office were in the basement of the courthouse. On occasion I waited for my father to release a prisoner (usually a hung-over drunk jailed so he wouldn't hurt himself) or finish tacking up a wanted poster before I showed him my report card or asked him for a dime for a movie. No, if there had been a six-shooter or a Stetson or a pair of hand-tooled cowboy boots around for my father to put on with his badge, I would have known about it. (I must correct that previous statement: my father never *wore* his badge; he carried it in his suit-coat or shirt pocket. I always believed that this was part of his self-effacing way, and that may be so. But now that the badge is mine—my mother sent it to me after my father's death and I have it pinned to my bulletin board—I realize there was another reason, connected not to character but to practicality. The badge, not star-shaped but a shield, is heavy and its pin as thick as a pencil's lead. My father would have been poking fair-sized holes in his suits and shirts, and the badge's weight could have torn fabric.)

If my father didn't fit my ideal of what he should be in his occupation, he certainly didn't fit my mother's either. She wanted him to be an attorney. Which he was; he graduated from the University of North Dakota Law School, and he was a member of both the North Dakota and Montana State Bar Associations. My mother fervently believed that my father—indeed, all of us—would be happier if he practiced law and if we did not live in Montana, and her reasons had little to do with the potentially hazardous nature of a sheriff's work compared to an attorney's or the pay scale along which those professions positioned themselves. She wanted my father to find another job and for us to move because only doing those things would, she felt, allow my father to be fully himself. Her contention is one I must explain.

My father was born in 1910 in Mercer County and grew up on a large cattle ranch outside Bentrock. In the early twenties my father, with his parents and his brother, moved to Bentrock, where my grandfather began his first of many terms as county sheriff. My grandfather kept the ranch and had it worked by hands while he was in office, and since Mercer County had a statute that a sheriff could serve only three consecutive terms, he was able to return to the ranch every six years. When Grandfather's terms expired, his deputy, Len McAuley, would serve a term; after Len's term, Grandfather would run again, and this way they kept the office in the proper hands. During his terms as sheriff, Grandfather brought his family into town to live in a small apartment above a bar (he owned the bar and building the apartment was in). My father often spoke of how difficult it was for him to move from the ranch and its open expanses to the tiny apartment that always smelled of stale beer and cigar smoke. He spent every weekend and every summer at the ranch and when he had to return to the apartment where he and his brother slept on a fold-out couch, he felt like crying.

(And now that it is too late to ask anyone, I wonder: Why did my grandfather first run for sheriff? This one I can probably answer, from my memory and knowledge of him. He wanted, he needed, power. He was a dominating man who drew sustenance and strength from controlling others. To him, being the law's agent probably seemed part of a natural progression—first you master the land and its beasts, then you regulate the behavior of men and women.)

When my grandfather finally decided to retire for good

and return to the ranch, he found a way to do this yet retain his power in the county: he turned the post over to my father. Yes, the sheriff of Mercer County was elected, but such was my grandfather's popularity and influence—and the weight of the Hayden name—that it was enough for my grandfather to say, as he had earlier said of his deputy, now I want my son to have this job.

So my father set aside his fledgling law practice and took the badge my grandfather offered. It would never have occurred to my father to refuse.

There you have it, then, a portrait of my father in those years, a man who tried to turn two ways at once—toward my grandfather, who wanted his son to continue the Hayden rule of Mercer County, and toward my mother, who wanted her husband to be merely himself and not a Hayden. That was not possible as long as we lived in my grandfather's domain.

There was another reason my mother wanted us to leave Montana for a tamer region and that reason had to do with me. My mother feared for my soul, a phrase that sounds to me now comically overblown, yet I remember that those were precisely the words she used.

My mother was concerned about my values, but since often the most ordinary worldly matters assumed for her a spiritual significance, she saw the problem as centered on my mortal being. (My mother was a Lutheran of boundless devotion; my father was irreligious, a path I eventually found and followed after wandering through those early years of church, Sunday School, and catechism classes.)

The problem was that I wanted to grow up wild. Oh, not

in the sense that wildness is used today. I wasn't particularly interested, on the cusp of adolesence, in driving fast cars (pickup trucks, more accurately in Bentrock), smoking (Sir Walter Raleigh roll-your-owns the cigarette of choice), drinking (home-brewed beer was so prevalent in Mercer County that boys always had access to it), or chasing girls (for some reason, the girls from farms—not town or ranch or reservation—had the reputation of being easy). In fact, I came late to these temptations.

Wildness meant, to me, getting out of town and into the country. Even our small town—really, in 1948 still a frontier town in many respects—tasted to me like pabulum. It stood for social order, good manners, the chimed schedules of school and church. It was a world meant for storekeepers, teachers, ministers, for the rule-makers, the order-givers, the law-enforcers. And in my case, my parents were not only figurative agents of the law, my father *was* the law.

In addition to my discomfort with the strictures of town (a common and natural reaction for a boy), I had another problem that seemed like mine alone. I never felt as though I understood how town life *worked*. I thought there was some secret knowledge about living comfortably and unself-consciously in a community, and I was sure I did not possess that knowledge. When the lessons were taught about how to feel confident and at ease in school, in stores, in cafes, with other children or adults, I must have been absent. It was not as though I behaved badly in these situations but rather that I was never sure how to behave. I was always looking sneakily at others for the key to correct conduct. And instead of attributing this social distress to my own shy and too-serious character I simply blamed life in town and sought to escape it as often as I could.

And that was an easy enough matter. Though we lived in the middle of town, I could be out in minutes, whether I walked, biked, ran, or followed the railroad tracks just on the other side of our backyard. With my friends or on my own, I spent as many of the day's hours as I could outdoors, usually out at my grandfather's ranch or along the banks of the Knife River. (How it got its name I've never known; it's hard to imagine a duller body of water—in dry summers it could barely keep its green course flowing and sandbars poked up the length of it; it froze every year by Thanksgiving.)

I did what boys usually did and exulted in the doing: I rode horseback (I had my own horse at the ranch, an unnaturally shaggy little sorrel named Nutty); I swam; I fished; I hunted (I still have, deep in a closet somewhere, my first guns from those years—a single-shot bolt action Winchester .22 and a single-shot Montgomery Ward .410 shotgun); my friends and I killed more beer cans, soda bottles, road signs, and tele-phone pole insulators than the rabbits, squirrels, grouse, or pheasants we said we were hunting; I explored; I scavenged (at various times I brought home a snakeskin, part of a cow's jawbone, an owl's coughball, a porcupine quill, the broken shaft and fletch of a hunter's arrow, an unbroken clay pigeon, a strip of tree bark with part of a squirrel's tail embedded in it so tightly that it was a mystery how it got there, a perfectly shaped cottonwood leaf the size of a man's hand, and a myriad of river rocks chosen for their beauty or odd shape).

23

But what I did was not important. Out of town I could simply *be*, I could feel my *self*, firm and calm and unmalleable as I could not when I was in school or in any of the usual human communities that seemed to weaken or scatter me. I could sit for an hour in the rocks above the Knife River, asking for no more discourse than that water's monotonous gabble. I was an inward child, it was true, but beyond that, I felt a contentment outside human society that I couldn't feel within it.

Perhaps my mother sensed this, and following her duty to civilize me, wished for a larger community to raise me in, one that I couldn't get out of quite so easily and that wouldn't offer such alluring chaos once I was out. (The impression is probably forming of my mother as an urban woman disposed by background to be suspicious of wild and rough Montana. Not so. She grew up on a farm in eastern North Dakota, in the Red River valley, flat, fertile, prosperous farming country.)

That was our family in 1948 and those were the tensions that set the air humming in our household. I need to sketch in only one more character and the story can begin.

Because my mother worked (she was the secretary in the Register of Deeds office, also in the courthouse across the street), we had a housekeeper who lived with us during the week. Her name was Marie Little Soldier, and she was a Hunkpapa Sioux who originally came from the Fort Berthold Reservation in North Dakota. She was in her early twenties, and she came to our part of Montana when her mother married a Canadian who owned a bar in Bentrock. The bar, Frenchy's, was a dirty, run-down cowboy hangout at the edge of town. Among my friends the rumor was that Frenchy kept locked in his storeroom a fat old toothless Indian woman whom anyone could have sex with for two dollars. (One of my friends hinted that this was Marie's mother, but I knew that wasn't true. Marie's mother once came to our house, and she was a thin, shy woman barely five feet tall. She reminded me of a bird who wants to be brave in the presence of humans but finally fails. When Marie introduced her to my mother, Marie's mother looked at the floor and couldn't say a word.)

Marie was neither small nor shy. She loved to laugh and talk, and she was a great tease, specializing in outrageous lies about everything from strange animal behavior to bloody murders. Then, as soon as she saw she had you gulled, she would say, "Not so, not so!"

She was close to six feet tall and though she wasn't exactly fat she had a fleshy amplitude about her that made her seem simultaneously soft and strong, as if all that body could be ready, at a moment's notice, for sex or work. The cotton print dresses she wore must have been handed down or up to her because they never fit her quite right; they were either too short and tight and she looked about to pop out of them, or they were much too large and she threatened to fall free or be tangled in all that loose fabric. She had a wide, pretty face and cheekbones so high, full, and glossy I often wondered if they were naturally like that or if they were puffy and swollen. Her hair was black and long and straight, and she was always pulling strands of it from the corner of her mouth or parting it to clear her vision.

And I loved her.

Because she talked to me, cared for me. . . . Because she

25

was older but not too old. . . . Because she was not as quiet and conventional as every other adult I knew. . . . Because she was sexy, though my love for her was, as a twelve-year-old's love often is, chaste.

Besides, Marie had a boyfriend, Ronnie Tall Bear, who worked on a ranch north of town. I was not jealous of Ronnie, because I liked him almost as much as I liked Marie. *Liked* Ronnie? I worshipped him. He had graduated from Bentrock High School a few years earlier, and he was one of the finest athletes the region had ever produced. He was the Mustangs' star fullback, the high-scoring forward in basketball; in track he set school records in the discus, javelin, and 400-yard dash. He pitched and played outfield on the American Legion baseball team. (I realize now how much I was a part of that era's thinking: I never wondered then, as I do now, why a college didn't snap up an athlete like Ronnie. Then, I knew without being told, as if it were knowledge that I drank in with the water, that college was not for Indians.) During the war Ronnie was in the infantry (good enough for the Army but not for college). Marie told me he was thinking of trying his hand on the rodeo circuit.

Marie's room, when she stayed with us during the week, was a small room off the kitchen. My bedroom and my parents' were on the second floor. (And as I go back in my memory I realize we had a third bedroom on the second floor. Who decided that room should not be Marie's? I had long known that I was destined to be an only child.) I mention Marie's room because it was there, and with her, that this story began.

26

It was mid-August 1948. Our corner of the state had been, as usual, hot and dry, though even in the midst of all the heat there were a few signs of autumn—a cottonwood leaf here and there turning yellow and sometimes letting go, and nights cool enough for a light blanket.

Marie stayed in her room all that morning, and when I passed the door I heard her coughing. I peered in once and saw her lying on the bed. She came out only long enough to set out lunch. At our house meals were never fancy, but the food was always abundant and varied. Marie probably brought out cottage cheese, perhaps some leftover ham or chicken or sausage, a wedge of cheddar cheese, a loaf of bread, butter, pickles, canned peaches, cold milk, and something from the garden— carrots or radishes or cucumbers or tomatoes.

The noon whistle blew and within five minutes my mother was walking through the door, and if my father was in town, he would soon follow.

I stopped my mother in the living room and whispered to her, "I think Marie's sick."

"What's wrong?" My mother was instantly alarmed. She feared nothing more than disease, but she was not cowardly or meek in its presence. No disease, common or exotic, faced a fiercer foe than my mother. She spent a good deal of energy avoiding it or keeping it away from herself and her family. She would not accept or extend invitations if she knew it meant someone sick might get too close. If we were walking down the street and someone ahead of us coughed or sneezed, my mother slowed her pace until she thought those germs had dissipated in the air. It all sounds silly, but it must have worked.

We were seldom sick, and I did not get the usual childhood diseases until I left home. (And then they hit me hard. I had to drop a French class my freshman year in college because measles laid me up and put me too far behind. Years later my fever ran so high when I had chicken pox that my wife took me to the emergency room, where they packed me in ice.)

"I'm not sure," I told my mother. "She's been in her room all morning."

My mother walked quietly through the living room and kitchen to the door of Marie's room. I followed close behind.

The door wasn't shut tight, and my mother knocked hard enough so it swung open. "Marie? Are you all right?"

Just then Marie had another coughing fit, and she couldn't answer. She rolled onto her side, brought her knees up, and barked out a series of dry coughs. When the spasm subsided, she nodded. "A cold. I have a little cold."

My mother would have none of it. She went to the bedside and put her hand on Marie's forehead. "Come here," my mother commanded me. When I came close, she put her hand on my forehead. The comparison confirmed what she suspected.

"You have a temperature, all right."

If my father had been there he would have been quick to correct my mother's choice of words. "A fever, Gail. She has a *fever*. Everyone has a temperature."

My mother gave my forehead a tiny little push as she took her hand away, a signal that I was supposed to get back—there was illness here.

I didn't go far. I stood in the doorway and watched Marie while my mother went through her routine of questions.

"How long have you been feeling sick?"

Marie rolled onto her back and brushed her hair from her face. Her cheeks now glowed so brightly they looked painful, as if they had been rubbed raw. Her eyes seemed darker than ever, all pupil, black water that swallowed light and gave nothing back. Her lips were pale-dry and chapped. Her dress had ridden up over her knees and the sight of her sturdy brown legs and bare feet was strangely shocking, a glimpse of the sensual in the sickroom. (But nothing new. I had once seen Marie naked, or nearly so. In our basement laundry room we had a shower, nothing fancy—a shower head, a tin stall, and an old green rubber curtain with large white sea horses on it. I came galloping downstairs one day—obviously when Marie thought I would be out of the house a while longer—and caught her just as she was stepping out of the shower. She was quick with her towel but not quick enough. I saw just enough to embarrass us both. Dark nipples that shocked me in the way they stood out like fingertips. A black triangle of pubic hair below a thick waist and gently rounded belly. And above it all, shoulders that seemed as broad as my father's. I stammered an apology and backed out as quickly as possible. Neither of us ever said anything about the incident.)

After another brief coughing fit, this time nothing more than some breathy, urgent *chuffs*, Marie answered, "I don't know. A couple days maybe."

"Have you been eating?"

Marie shook her head.

"Are you sick to your stomach?"

Another head shake.

"Have you been throwing up?"

Marie whispered no.

"Do you know anyone else who is sick? Someone you might have caught this from?"

I felt so bad for Marie having to put up with this interrogation that I finally said something. "Mom. She doesn't feel good."

My mother turned and said sharply, "You wait in the other room. I'm trying to find out something here."

I took a few steps back into the kitchen, but I still saw and heard what went on in Marie's room.

My mother brought two wool blankets down from the closet shelf and spread them over Marie. "The first thing," my mother said, "is to bring your temperature down. We should be able to sweat that out of you in no time."

To this day many Sioux practice a kind of purification ritual in which they enclose themselves in a small tent or lodge and with the help of heated stones and water steam themselves until sweat streams from them. My mother believed in a variation of that. A fever was to be driven away by more heat, blankets piled on until your own sweat cooled you.

Marie must have agreed with the course of treatment because she made no protest.

"David will be here this afternoon if you need anything," my mother said. "You rest. I'll come over again around three o'clock, and if you're not feeling better we'll give Dr. Hayden a call."

This remark brought Marie straight up in bed. "No! I don't

30

need no doctor!" With that outburst she began coughing again, this time harder than ever.

"Listen to you," my mother said. "Listen to that cough. And you say you don't need a doctor."

"I don't go to him," said Marie. "I go to Dr. Snow."

"Dr. Hayden is Mr. Hayden's brother. You know that, don't you? He'll come to the house. And he won't charge anything, if that's what you're worried about." Marie's frugality was legendary. She hated waste, and on more than a few occasions she claimed what we were going to throw away—food, clothing, magazines—saying she would find a use for them. Finally we caught on. Before we planned to throw anything away, we checked with Marie first. Our old issues of *Collier's* probably found their way out to the reservation.

Marie closed her eyes. "I don't need no doctor." Her voice was no louder than a whisper.

My mother left the room, closing the door halfway. "Keep an eye on her, David," she told me. "If she gets worse, call me."

"Is she very sick?"

"She has a temperature. And I don't like the sound of that cough."

I stayed out, as my mother ordered, but I walked past Marie's room often. Marie slept, even when she coughed. I heard her voice on one of my passings and stopped, but it soon became obvious that she was not calling me but talking in her fevered sleep. "It's the big dog," she said. "Yellow dog. It won't drink." And then a word that sounded like *ratchety*. And repeated, "Ratchety, ratchety." I didn't know if it was a word from Sioux or from fever.

Later, as I was sitting at the kitchen table, Marie shouted for me. "Davy!" I ran to her door.

I stopped. Marie was lying on her back, gazing at the doorway. "I don't need no doctor, Davy. Tell them."

"My mom doesn't want you to get worse."

"No *doctor*."

"It's just my uncle Frank. He's okay."

Marie's forehead and cheeks shone with sweat. "I'm feeling better," she said. She pulled back the blankets and sat up, but as she did she began to cough again. Soon she was gasping for breath in between coughs. This frightened me. I went to the bed and held Marie's shoulders until the coughing subsided, something I remembered my mother doing for me. I felt Marie trembling all over, as your muscles do after great exertion.

When she was done I helped her lie down again. "Maybe I should go get my mother."

"No doctor."

"Okay, okay. I'll tell her you don't want a doctor."

Marie's eyes closed and she seemed to be breathing evenly again.

"Marie?"

She nodded weakly. "I'm okay."

I backed slowly away but hesitated in the doorway. Marie's eyes remained closed and her breathing was deep and regular. My hands were damp from gripping Marie's shoulders. Was the sweat mine or hers?

My mother and father came home together at five o'clock. If the evening followed its usual pattern, my father would read the *Mercer County Gazette*, have supper, and go out again for an hour or two if the evening was peaceful. He would be gone longer if it was not.

My father dropped his hat and briefcase (another lawyer's touch—and a gift from my mother) on the kitchen table. "David," he said, "I hear you're baby-sitting the baby-sitter."

How naive I was! Until that moment I believed that we had hired Marie to care for our house, to keep it clean and prepare the meals since my mother, unlike most mothers, worked all day outside our home. We called Marie our "housekeeper," and I thought that was her job—to keep the house. It never occurred to me that she had been hired to look after me as well.

My mother headed for Marie's room.

"I think she's still sleeping," I said.

Within minutes my mother came back out. She said, "She's burning up, Wes. You'd better call Frank."

My father did not question my mother's judgment in these matters. He went for the phone.

"Wait!" I called.

Both my father and mother turned to me. I did not often demand my parents' attention because I knew I could have it whenever I wanted it. That was part of my only-child legacy.

"Marie said she didn't want a doctor."

"That's superstition, David," said my father. "Indian superstition."

This is as good a place as any to mention something that I would just as soon forget. My father did not like Indians. No, that's not exactly accurate, because it implies that my father disliked Indians, which wasn't so. He simply held them in low regard. He was not a hate-filled bigot—he probably thought he was free of prejudice!—and he could treat Indians with generosity, kindness, and respect (as he could treat every human being). Nevertheless, he believed Indians, with only a few exceptions, were ignorant, lazy, superstitious, and irresponsible. I first learned of his racism when I was seven or eight. An aunt gave me a pair of moccasins for my birthday, and my father forbade me to wear them. When I made a fuss and my mother sided with me, my father said, "He wears those and soon he'll be as flat-footed and lazy as an Indian." My mother gave in by supposing that he was right about flat feet. (Today I put on a pair of moccasins as soon as I come home from work, an obedient son's belated, small act of defiance.)

"She said she doesn't need one," I said.

"What does she need, David? A medicine man?"

I shut up. Both my parents were capable of scorching sarcasm. I saw no reason to risk receiving any more of it.

My father was already on the phone, giving the operator my uncle's home phone number. "Glo?" he said into the receiver. "This is Wes. Is the doctor home yet?" Gloria, my uncle's wife, was the prettiest woman I had ever seen.

34

(Prettier even than my mother—a significant admission for a boy to make.) Aunt Gloria was barely five feet tall, and she had silver-blond hair. She and Frank had been married five or six years but had no children. I once overheard my grandfather say to my uncle: "Is she too small to have kids? Is that it, Frank? Is the chute too tight?"

In the too-loud voice he always used on the telephone, my father said, "We've got a sick Indian girl over here, Frank. Gail wants to know if you can stop by."

After a pause, my father said to my mother, "Frank wants to know what her symptoms are."

"A high temperature. Chills. Coughing."

My father repeated my mother's words. Then he added, "I might as well tell you, Frank. She doesn't want to see you. Says she doesn't need a doctor."

Another short pause and my father said, "She didn't say why. My guess is she's never been to anyone but the tribal medicine man."

I couldn't tell if my father was serious or making a joke.

He laughed and hung up the phone. "Frank said maybe he'd do a little dance around the bed. And if that doesn't work he'll try beating some drums."

My mother didn't laugh. "I'll go back in with Marie."

As soon as Uncle Frank arrived, his tie loosened and his sleeves rolled up, I felt sorry for my father. It was the way I always felt when the two of them were together. Brothers naturally invite comparison, and when comparisons were made between those two, my father was bound to suffer. And my father was, in many respects, an impressive man. He was tall, broad-shouldered, and pleasant-looking. But Frank was all this and more. He was handsome—dark, wavy hair, a jaw chiseled on such precise angles it seemed to conform to some geometric law, and he was as tall and well built as my father, but with an athletic grace my father lacked. He had been a star athlete in high school and college, and he was a genuine war hero, complete with decorations and commendations. He had been stationed at an Army field hospital on a Pacific island, and during a battle in which Allied forces were incurring a great many losses, Uncle Frank left the hospital to assist in treating and evacuating casualties. Under heavy enemy fire he carried—carried, just like in the movies—three wounded soldiers from the battlefield to safety. The story made the wire services, and somehow my grandfather got ahold of clippings from close to twenty different newspapers. (After reading one of the clippings, my father muttered, "I wonder if he was supposed to stay at the hospital.")

Frank was witty, charming, at smiling ease with his life and everything in it. Alongside his brother my father soon seemed somewhat prosaic. Oh, stolid, surely, and steady and dependable. But inevitably, inescapably dull. Nothing glittered in my father's wake the way it did in Uncle Frank's.

Soon after the end of the war the town held a picnic to celebrate his homecoming. (Ostensibly the occasion was to honor all returning veterans, but really it was for Uncle Frank.) The park was jammed that day (I'm sure no event has ever gathered as many of the county's residents in one place), and the amount and variety of food, all donated, was amazing: a roast pig, a barbecued side of beef, pots of beans, brimming bowls of coleslaw and potato salad, an array of garden vegetables, freshly baked pies and cakes, and pitchers of lemonade, urns of coffee, and barrels of beer. Once people had eaten and drunk their fill, my grandfather climbed onto a picnic table.

He didn't call for silence. That wasn't his way. He simply stood there, his feet planted wide, his hands on his hips. He was wearing his long buckskin jacket, the one so tanned and aged that it was almost white. He assumed that once people saw him, they would give him their attention. And they did.

He said a few words honoring all the men who served (no one from Mercer County was killed in action—not such an improbability when you consider the county's small population—though we had our share of wounded, the worst of whom, Harold Branch, came back without his legs). Then after a long, reverent pause, Grandfather announced, "Now I'd like to bring my son up here."

My father was standing next to me when Grandfather said that. My father did not move. Grandfather did not say, "my son the veteran," or "my son the war hero," or "my son the soldier." He simply said, "my son." And why wouldn't the county sheriff be called on to make a small speech?

But my father didn't move. He just stood there, like every other man in the crowd, smiling and applauding, while his brother stepped up on the table. Uncle Frank had not hesitated either; he knew immediately that Grandfather was referring to him.

37

Uncle Frank made a suitably brief and modest speech, saying that the war could not have been won without the sacrifices of both soldiers and those who remained at home.

At one point I looked up to see how my father was reacting to his brother's speech. My father was not there. He had drifted back through the crowd and was picking up scraps of paper from the grass. With his bad leg, bending was difficult. He had to keep the leg stiff and bend from the waist. Then he carried these bits of paper, a piece at a time, to the fire-blackened incinerator barrel.

Uncle Frank's talk must not have been enough for my grandfather. He climbed back up on the table and, after urging the crowd on to another minute of applause, held up his hands for silence again. "This man could have gone anywhere," he said. "With his war record he could be practicing in Billings. In Denver. In *Los Angeles*. There's not a community in the country that wouldn't be proud to have him. But he came back to us. My son. *Came back to us*."

My father kept searching for paper to pick up.

Uncle Frank put his black bag on the kitchen table. "How about something to drink, Wes? I was digging postholes this morning and I've been dry all day."

My father opened the refrigerator. "Postholes? Not exactly the kind of surgery I thought you'd be doing."

"I'm going to fence off the backyard. We've got two more

houses going up out there. Figured a fence might help us keep what little privacy we've got."

I wondered what Grandpa Hayden would say about that. Though his land was fenced with barbed wire as most ranchers' were, he still had the nineteenth-century cattleman's open range mentality and hatred of fences. Our backyard bordered a railroad track (trains passed at least four times a day), but my father refused to put up a fence—as all our neighbors had—separating our property from the tracks.

"I've got cold beer in here," said my father. "It's old man Norgaard's brew." Ole Norgaard lived in a tar-paper shack on the edge of town. He had a huge garden and sold vegetables through the summer and early fall. His true specialty, however, and the business he conducted throughout the year, was brewing and selling beer. My father swore by everything Ole Norgaard produced.

Uncle Frank made a face. "I'll pass."

My father brought out a bottle with a rubber stopper and a wire holding it in place. "You can't buy a better beer." He held out the bottle.

Uncle Frank laughed and waved my father away. "Just give me a glass of water."

My father persisted. "Ask Pop. He still drinks Ole Norgaard's beer."

"Okay, okay," Frank said. "It's great beer. It's the world's greatest goddamn beer. But I'll drink Schlitz, if it's okay with you."

My father nodded in my direction. "Not in front of the

boy." That was one of my father's rules: no one was supposed to swear in front of my mother or me.

Uncle Frank picked up his bag. "Okay, Wes. I'll tell you what. Let me see the patient first and then I'll drink a bottle of Ole's beer with you. Maybe I'll drink two."

Just then my mother came out of Marie's room. "She's in here, Frank."

"Hello, Gail. How is the patient?"

"She's awake. Her temperature might be down a bit."

Frank went in and shut the door behind him. Within a minute we heard Marie shouting, "Mrs.! Mrs.!"

My mother looked quizzically at my father. He shrugged his shoulders. Marie screamed again. "No! Mrs.!"

This time my mother went to the door and knocked. "Frank? Is everything okay?"

My uncle opened the door. "She says she wants you in here, Gail." He shook his head in disgust. "Come on in. I don't give a damn."

This time the door closed and the room remained silent.

"David," my father said to me. "Why don't we go out on the porch while the medical profession does its work."

Our screened-in porch faced the courthouse across the street. When I was younger I used to go out there just before five o'clock on all but the coldest days to watch for my parents.

My father put his bottle of beer down on the table next to the rocking chair. I didn't sit down; I wanted to be able to maneuver myself into the best position to hear anything coming from Marie's room. I didn't have to wait long. I soon heard—muffled but unmistakable—Marie shout another *no*.

I glanced at my father but he was staring at the courthouse.

Then two more *no*'s in quick-shouted succession.

My father pointed at one of the large elm trees in our front yard. "Look at that," he said. "August, and we've got leaves coming down already." He heard her. I knew he did.

Before long Uncle Frank came out to the porch. He put down his bag and stared around the room as if he had never been there before. "Nice and cool out here," he said, tugging at his white shirt the way men do when their clothes are sticking to them from perspiration. "Maybe I should put up one of these."

"Faces east," my father said. "That's the key."

"I'll drink that beer now."

My father jumped up immediately.

Uncle Frank lowered his head and closed his eyes. He pinched the bridge of his nose and worked his fingers back and forth as if he were trying to straighten his nose. I heard the smack of the refrigerator door and the clink of bottles. I wanted my father to hurry. After what had just happened with Marie I didn't want to be alone with Uncle Frank.

Without opening his eyes Frank asked, "You playing any ball this summer, David?"

I was reluctant to answer. My uncle Frank had been a local baseball star, even playing some semipro ball during the summers when he was in college and medical school. I, on the other hand, had been such an inept ball player that I had all but given it up. But since Frank and Gloria had no children I always felt some pressure to please them, to be like the son they didn't have. I finally said, "I've been doing a lot of fishing."

"Catching anything?"

"Crappies and bluegill and perch out at the lake. Some trout at the river."

"Any size to the trout?" He finally looked up at me.

"Not really. Nine inches. Maybe a couple twelve-inchers."

"Well, that's pan size. You'll have to take me out some afternoon."

Before I could answer, my father returned, carrying a bottle of beer. "Now drink it slow," he said. "Give it a chance."

Frank made a big show of holding the bottle aloft and examining it before drinking.

"What was the problem with Marie?" asked my father.

"Like you said on the phone. They're used to being treated by the medicine man. Or some old squaw. But a doctor comes around and they think he's the evil spirit or something."

My father shook his head. "They're not going to make it into the twentieth century until they give up their superstitions and old ways."

"I'm not concerned about social progress. I'm worried they're not going to survive measles. Mumps. Pneumonia. Which is what Marie might have. I'd like to get an X-ray, but I don't suppose there's much chance of that."

"Pneumonia," said my father. "That sounds serious."

"I can't be sure. I'll prescribe something just in case."

From where I stood on the porch I could see into the living room, where my mother stood. She was staring toward the porch and standing absolutely still. Her hands were pressed

42

together as they would be in prayer, but she held her hands to her mouth. I looked quickly behind me since her attitude was exactly like someone who has seen something frightening. Nothing was there but my father and my uncle.

"Should she be in the hospital?" asked my father.

Frank rephrased the question as if my father had somehow said it wrong. "*Should* she be? That depends. Would she stay there? Or would she sneak out? Would she go home? If she's going to be in some dirty shack out on the prairie, that's no good. Now if she were staying right here. . . ."

Bentrock did not have its own hospital. The nearest one was almost forty miles away, in North Dakota. Bentrock residents usually traveled an extra twenty miles to the hospital in Dixon, Montana.

My mother came out onto the porch to answer Frank's question. "Yes, she's staying here. She's staying until she gets better." Her voice was firm and her arms were crossed, almost as if she expected an argument.

"Or until she gets worse. You don't want an Indian girl with pneumonia in your house, Gail."

"As long as she's here we can keep an eye on her."

Frank looked over at my father. If my mother said it, it was so, yet my father's confirmation was still necessary. "She can stay here," he said.

"She's staying *here*," my mother said one more time. "Someone will be here or nearby."

I couldn't figure out why my mother seemed so angry. I had always felt she didn't particularly care for Frank, but I had put that down to two reasons. First, he was charming, and my

43

mother was suspicious of charm. She believed its purpose was to conceal some personal deficit or lack of substance. If your character was sound, you didn't need charm. And second, Uncle Frank was a Hayden, and where the Haydens were concerned my mother always held something back.

Yet her comportment toward Frank had always been cordial if a little reserved. My parents and Frank and Gloria went out together; they met at least once a month to play cards; they saw each other regularly at the ranch at holidays and family gatherings. When either my father or I were hurt or fell ill, we went to see Frank or he came to see us. (My mother, however, went to old Dr. Snow, the other doctor in Bentrock. She said she would feel funny seeing Frank professionally.)

Whatever the source of her irritation, Frank must have felt it too. He abruptly put down his half-finished beer and said, "I'd better be on my way. I have the feeling I might be called out to the Hollands tonight. This is her due date, and she's usually pretty close. I'll phone Young Drug with something for Marie. Give me a call if she gets worse."

The three of us watched Frank bound down the walk, his long strides loose yet purposeful. After he got into his old Ford pickup (an affectation that my father made fun of by saying "If a doctor is going to drive an old truck, maybe I should be patrolling the streets on horseback") and drove away, my mother suggested I go outside. "I have to talk to your father," she said. "In private."

If I had gone back into the house—to the kitchen, to my room, out the back door, if I had left the porch and followed Frank's steps down the front walk—I would never have heard

44

the conversation between my father and mother, and perhaps I would have lived out my life with an illusion about my family and perhaps even the human community. Certainly I could not tell this story. . . .

I left the porch and turned to the right and went around the corner of the house. From there I was able to crouch down and double back to the side of the porch, staying below the screen and out of my parents' line of vision. I knew my mother was going to say something about Marie yelling when Uncle Frank was there, and I wanted to hear what she had to say.

I didn't have to wait long.

My mother cleared her throat, and when she began to speak, her voice was steady and strong, but her pauses were off, as if she had started on the wrong breath. "The reason, Wesley, the reason Marie didn't want to be examined by Frank is that he—he has . . . is that your brother has molested Indian girls."

My father must have started to leave because I heard the clump of a heavy footstep and my mother said quickly, "No, wait. Listen to me, please. Marie said she didn't want to be alone with him. You should have seen her. She was practically hysterical about having me stay in the room. And once Frank left she told me all of it. He's been doing it for years, Wes. When he examines an Indian he . . . he does things he shouldn't. He takes liberties. Indecent liberties."

There was a long silence. My mother's hollyhocks and snapdragons grew alongside the house where I was hiding, and the bees that flew in and out of the flowers filled the air with their drone.

Then my father spoke. "And you believe her."

"Yes, I do."

Footsteps again. Now I knew my father was pacing.

"Why would she lie, Wesley?"

My father didn't say anything, but I knew what he was thinking: She's an Indian—why would she tell the truth?

"Why, Wes?"

"I didn't say she was lying. Maybe she's simply got it wrong. An examination by a doctor. . . . Maybe she doesn't know what's supposed to go on. My gosh, I remember when I had to go see Doc Snow for my school checkups. He would poke me and tickle me and check my testicles and have me cough, and I might have felt funny about the whole business, but I knew it was part of the exam. But if I *didn't* know and. . . ."

"It's not like that. Marie told me. That's not the case."

"And if you'd never seen a doctor in your life. . . . Why, you wouldn't know what was going on."

"No, Wes."

"Think if you'd never had a shot, an injection. If you'd never seen a needle. You'd think he was trying to kill you. To stab you."

"Wesley, would you *listen* to me?"

"And Marie. For God's sake, you know how she likes to make up stories. She's been filling David's head with them for years. She's got a great sense of drama, that one—"

"*Wesley!*" My mother shouted my father's name exactly the way she would shout a baby's to stop him from doing something dangerous—toddling toward the stairs, extending his

46

finger toward the electrical outlet—anything to stop him. I flinched and a part of me said leave, get away, run, now before it's too late, before you hear something you can't unhear. Before everything changes. But I pressed myself closer to the house and hung on.

"All right," my father said. "All right. Let's have it."

There was a shuffling, and I wondered if my mother was moving closer to my father. Her voice became lower. "I told you. When he examines Indian girls he does things to them."

"Things, Gail? He does *things* to them? I'm sure he does *things* to all his patients."

His tone must have angered her, because her voice went right back to where it had been earlier, and though it seemed each word was the product of effort it also seemed born out of absolute determination. "What things? I'll tell you what things. Your brother makes his patients—*some* of his patients—undress completely and get into indecent positions. He makes them jump up and down while he watches. He fondles their breasts. He—no, don't you turn away. *Don't!* You asked and I'm going to tell you. All of it. He puts things into these girls. Inside them, *there.* His instruments. His fingers. He has . . . your brother I believe has inserted his, his penis into some of these girls. Wesley, your brother is *raping* these women. These *girls.* These Indian girls. He offers his services to the reservation, to the BIA school. To the high school for athletic physicals. Then when he gets these girls where he wants them. . . . *Oh!* I don't even want to say it again. *He does what he wants to do.*"

The shock of hearing this about Uncle Frank was doubled

47

because my mother was saying these words. *Rape. Breasts. Penis.* These were words I never heard my mother use— never—and I'm sure her stammer was not only from emotion but also from the strain on her vocabulary.

I waited for my father to explode, to shout a defense of his brother, to scream a condemnation of Marie and her lies. Instead, he said as quietly as before: "Why are you telling me this?"

"*Why?*"

"That's right. Why? Are you telling me this because I'm Frank's brother? Because I'm your husband? Because I'm Marie's employer?" He paused. "Or because I'm the sheriff?"

"I'm telling *you,* Wes. I'm just telling *you.* Why? What part of you doesn't want to hear it?"

"I wish," my father said, "I wish you wouldn't have told the sheriff."

Did he laugh softly, ironically, then? I thought I heard a chuckling noise, but it might have been the heavy heads of the snapdragons leaning and rustling against each other.

Neither of them spoke for a long time. I wanted to stand up, to look at them. Were they embracing? Glaring at each other? For some reason I imagined them staring off in different directions, my father toward the front lawn and the leaves that fell before they should and my mother the other way, back into the house and toward the bedroom where Marie lay sweating in her fever and her shame.

My father asked, "Did any of this happen to Marie?"

"Yes. Some. Not the worst. But her friends. People she knows."

48

"Would she be willing to talk to me?"

"She might be. If you approach her the right way."

"I only have the one way."

"I know," my mother said.

My father clapped his hands, his usual prelude to action— time to put up the storm windows, to rake the leaves, to shovel the walk, to shake the rugs. To this day, when I hear the first clap of applause in a theater, a lecture hall, a banquet, I reflexively think of my father and his call to chores. "Let's see if she's awake," he said, "and get on with it."

As they left the porch, I ran around the house and went in the back door just as they were heading into Marie's room. Neither of them said a word to me. They went in and closed the door behind them. I lingered nearby but couldn't make out a word, only the steady low murmur of voices punctuated occasionally by Marie's coughs.

On the kitchen table was Uncle Frank's beer bottle. I examined it closely, searching for the lines and whorls of his fingerprints. (One of the ways my father kept the respect and admiration of the boys in our town during the war was by fingerprinting every child who stopped by his office. I must have been fingerprinted fifteen times myself.) I was beginning already to think of Uncle Frank as a criminal. I may not have been entirely convinced of his guilt, but the story my mother told was too lurid, too frightening, for me to continue thinking of my uncle in the way I always had. Charming, affable Uncle Frank was gone for good.

My parents were in Marie's room for a long time, and when they came out both of them were grim-faced and silent.

"How's Marie?" I asked my mother.

"She's going to sleep a while. That's what she needs now."

Our supper was soup and sandwiches, a meal usually reserved for lunches or Sunday evenings when we got home late from spending the day at the ranch. After eating, my father went back out on the porch and simply stood there, staring out at the evening's lengthening shadows. My mother was finishing the dishes when he came back in and announced, "I'm going over to talk to Len."

Len McAuley was my father's deputy and our next-door neighbor, and before he was my father's deputy he had been my grandfather's deputy. I once heard a story about how Len, without a weapon, ran down on foot and disarmed a cowboy who shot up a bar on Main Street, but the story was hard to believe about the Len McAuley I knew. He was tall, gaunt, stoop-shouldered, shy, and soft-spoken. Len and his wife Daisy (who made up for Len's taciturnity with both the quantity and the volume of her talk) were in their sixties, and they were more like grandparents to me than my own. When I was younger, Len used to carve little animals for my play, and Daisy never stopped baking cookies for me.

As my father went out the door, my mother called after him, "If Daisy's home tell her I've got a fresh pot of coffee!"

Moments later they were off on their own, my father and Len standing in the McAuley front yard and my mother and Daisy sitting at our kitchen table. But there were similarities. All four were drinking coffee. In each pair one talked while the other listened. (My mother and Len were the listeners.) And both my father and mother were, I knew, conducting investigations.

I wandered in and out of the house, catching fragments of both conversations, until my mother finally said, "David. Either go out or stay in." Daisy laughed and said, "He's like Cuss"—her cat—"when he's out, he wants to go in. When he's in he wants to go out."

Both my parents were discreet about their investigations. Neither came right out and repeated Marie's story about Uncle Frank, yet they used the same strategy: to mention Marie's perturbation and then to pretend mystification—"I don't know why she would act that way," my mother said, while my father shook his head in puzzlement. They both left openings for Len or Daisy to contribute what they could.

And my mother struck pay dirt.

On one of my passes through the kitchen, Daisy was hunched over the table, her white hair bobbing in my mother's direction and her tanned plump arm reaching toward my mother. Daisy's usually loud, brassy voice was lowered, but I heard her say, "The word is he doesn't do everything on the up-and-up." Then she noticed me. She straightened up and smiled at me but stopped talking. That meant I was supposed to leave the room, and I did. But slowly. As I crossed into the living room, Daisy whispered, "Just the squaws though."

Later that night, right before we all went to bed, my

mother checked on Marie once more. When she came out my father and I were in the kitchen, drinking milk and eating the rhubarb cake that Daisy had brought over.

My mother shut Marie's door quietly and then leaned her back against it, almost as if she were using her weight to keep the door closed. She looked tired. She was still wearing her work clothes—she usually changed into dungarees or slacks and a gingham shirt as soon as she got home. Her glasses were off and her eyes were ringed with fatigue. Her lipstick had faded, and she hadn't brushed out her hair.

My father asked without looking up, "How's Marie?"

My mother's gaze was fixed upon my father. "You're eating," she said.

"Daisy's cake. It's delicious."

"You can eat. . . ."

At some point my father must have become aware that she was staring at him. His cake unfinished, he set down his fork. "I don't hear her coughing."

"She's sleeping again." I couldn't tell if she was actually looking at him or if she was simply staring off and his form intersected her vision.

Then I knew. She saw him now as she hadn't before. He was not only her husband, he was a *brother,* and brother to a man who used his profession to take advantage of women, brother to a *pervert!* And how did I know these were my mother's thoughts? I knew because they were mine. I put down my glass of milk but I did not look at my father. I didn't want to notice the way he combed his hair straight back. I didn't want to see the little extra mound of flesh between his eyebrows. I didn't want to see the way the long line of his nose was interrupted by a slight inward curve. I didn't want to see any of the ways that he resembled his brother.

"What did Len say?" asked my mother.

"That we need rain."

My mother hung her head.

"That's what we talked about, Gail."

She brought her head up quickly. "That's not what Daisy and I talked about."

"I don't want this all over town, Gail. We don't have proof of anything."

Now they were falling into familiar roles. My father believed in *proof,* in evidence, and he held off on his own convictions until he had sufficient evidence to support them. My mother, on the other hand, was willing to go on a lot less, on her feelings, her faith.

My mother said, "It's around town more than you realize."

"I don't want this getting back to my father."

*That* was what my father believed in. If he could not sufficiently fear, love, trust, obey, and honor God—as we were told in catechism class we must—it was because he had nothing left for his Heavenly Father after declaring absolute fealty to his earthly one.

"Is that what you're concerned about?"

"Gail. . . ."

My mother pointed at me. "He won't be going to him again. I guarantee that."

"For God's sake, Gail."

"He *won't.*"

I was afraid I would give myself away—by blushing or failing to react the way I should. I wasn't supposed to know what they were talking about.

"Let's not discuss this in front of him."

My mother continued to stare at him.

"I'll handle this, Gail. In my fashion."

After another long silence, my mother finally left her post at Marie's door. She was almost out of the kitchen when she turned and said to my father in the calmest voice she had used all evening: "Just one thing, Wes. You never said you didn't believe it. Why is that? Why?"

She waited for his answer. I waited too, breathlessly, looking down at our floor's speckled linoleum and holding my sight on one green speck until my father said, of course I don't believe it; of course it isn't true.

But he didn't say a word. He simply picked up his fork and continued to eat Daisy McAuley's rhubarb cake.

That was when it came to me. Uncle Frank was my father's brother, and my father knew him as well as any man or woman.

And my father knew he was guilty.

# Two

✿ ✿ ✿

THE next day my father began investigating the accusation Marie had made against his brother. How did I know this? I made my guess from three facts. Before he left for his office in the morning he asked my mother if she needed any honey. He was driving out to the reservation, and if she liked he could stop at Birdwells' and buy her some honey. My mother had a passion for honey. She spread it on toast and biscuits; she sweetened her tea with it; she used it in baking; she ate spoonfuls of it right from the jar. And the best honey, she said, came from the Birdwells' bee farm. Mr. Birdwell's place was on the highway that led to the reservation.

My father's inquiry about the honey was, first of all, an overture of peace to my mother. Let's not quarrel, my father was saying. (The phrase he often used with both my mother and me was, "Let's not have this unpleasantness between us," as if the problem, whatever it might be, resided not *in* us but *outside* of us.)

And, second, the offer to buy honey was also an offhand way for my father to announce that he was going out to the reservation. He had no jurisdiction there, and the reservation police hadn't called him in on a case, so he could be going there for only one reason: to look into the accusations Marie had made.

Later that day I saw my father at the Coffee Cup, a popular diner in downtown Bentrock. There was nothing uncommon about my father (or any other citizen) being in the Coffee Cup on a summer afternoon, but my father usually sat at the large table in the center of the cafe, drinking coffee with his regular group: Don Young, the pharmacist; Rand Hutchinson, the owner of Hutchinson's Greenhouse; Howard Bailey, who ran an oil abstracting company; and other members of the Bentrock business community. On that day, however, he sat at a table for two over against the far wall. With him sat Ollie Young Bear, the most respected—even beloved—Indian in northeastern Montana, perhaps even the whole state.

Ollie Young Bear was also a war hero (he was wounded in action in North Africa), a graduate of Montana State University in Bozeman, a deacon at First Lutheran Church, an executive with Montana-Dakota Utilities Company, the star pitcher on the Elks' fast-pitch softball team—runner-up in the Silver Division of the state tournament (though he probably could not have been admitted to the Elks as a member). He did not smoke, drink, or curse. He married Doris Strickland, a white woman whose family owned a prosperous ranch south of Bentrock, and Ollie and Doris had two shy, polite children, a boy and a girl. All of these accomplishments made Ollie the perfect choice for white people to point to as an example of what Indians *could* be. My father liked to say of Ollie Young Bear, "He's a testimony to what hard work will get you."

And it was not as though Ollie had forsaken his own

people. Though he was not from the reservation, he drove out there every weekend with bats and balls, equipment he paid for out of his own pocket, and organized baseball games for the boys.

Because my father obviously liked and respected him— held him up, in fact, as a model—I tried to feel the same way about him. But it was difficult.

Mr. Young Bear, as my father insisted I call him, was a stern, censorious man. He was physically imposing—tall, barrel-chested, broad-shouldered, large-headed—and he never smiled. His lips were perpetually turned down in an expression both sad and disdainful. He seemed to find no humor in the world, and I have no memory of hearing him laugh.

He and my father went bowling together, and I was sometimes allowed to tag along. I didn't particularly care for the sport, but I loved Castle's Bowling Alley, a dark, narrow (only four lanes), low-ceilinged basement establishment that smelled of cigar smoke and floor wax. I loved to put my bottle of Nehi grape soda right next to my father's beer bottle on the scorecard holder and to slide my shoes under the bench with my father's when we changed into bowling shoes. I loved the sounds, the heavy clunk of the ball dropped on wood, its rumble down the alley, the clatter of pins, and above it all, men's shouts—"Go, go, gogogo!" "Get *in* there!" "Drop, *drop!*" Then the muttered curses while they waited for the pin boy to reset the pins. When I was in Castle's Alley I felt, no matter how many women or children might also be there, as though I had gained admittance to a men's enclave, as though I had *arrived*.

When Ollie Young Bear was with us, however, I felt like a

child. Ollie could not keep from giving me instruction or correcting my game. Make sure you bring the ball straight back, he would say. Follow through. Use a five-step approach, keep your eye on the spot and not the pins. He was relentless in his criticism, and my father would simply say, "Now listen to what Ollie's telling you. Do you know what kind of average he's carrying in league play? Two-ten. You listen to what he's telling you." I know my father was trying to show his esteem for Ollie and his lack of prejudice, but the only thing that was accomplished was that going bowling began to seem an awful lot like going to school.

When I saw my father and Ollie Young Bear sitting together at a table away from the others in the cafe, I knew my father was asking Ollie if he had heard anything about Uncle Frank molesting Indian girls. Was he asking the right man? I wondered. Although Ollie Young Bear was much admired by the white population, he had no special status among the Indians. In fact, I once heard Marie say of Ollie, "He won't be happy until he's white." Both Ollie and my father leaned over the table, their coffee cups between them, their voices low.

I left my friends at the counter and crossed the room to say hello to my father.

As I walked toward them, Ollie Young Bear was the first to notice me. He stopped talking and sat up straight, and then both of them stared at me. Neither smiled nor gave any sign of recognition, and I felt as if I were moving down a long chute, as if I were livestock, a horse, a sheep, a calf, being inspected as I walked. At that moment I knew that as long as this business was going on with his brother, my father had no use for a son. I could come and go as I wished; he wasn't about to notice me.

When I got to the table, my father said, "What can I do for you, David?"

By way of explanation I pointed to my friends at the counter. "We were fishing. . . ."

My father reached for his billfold. "You need some money."

"No, that's okay." I backed away. "I just wanted to say hi."

He managed a smile. "Are you going home? Look in on Marie, will you? Make sure she's taken her medicine."

When I got home Marie's door was open slightly but she was sleeping, as she almost always seemed to be since she'd gotten sick. Her bottle of pills and a glass of water were beside the bed, so I assumed she had taken what she was supposed to. I didn't want to wake her.

I was in the house for a few minutes when I felt something was wrong, yet I wasn't sure what it was. Then it struck me. It was the silence.

On our kitchen counter was a small Philco radio, its once-shining wood case now dull and riven with tiny hairline cracks in the varnish (on the top there was a darker brown ring where something—either a tube inside or a hot object out-side—had burned a perfect circle). The radio wasn't on and probably hadn't been for a couple days, and when Marie was there she always had the radio on, usually tuned to a Canadian

61

station that played Big Band music. To this day when I hear one of those television commercials urging us to send in $19.95 to get all the hits of the Big Band era—The Glen Miller Band, Artie Shaw and His Orchestra, Paul Whiteman, Kay Kaiser, Duke Ellington—or when I hear even a few bars of that music—"String of Pearls," "Tuxedo Junction," "Satin Doll"—I think of Marie. But I do not send my money in. My memories are strong enough—and painful enough—without prodding them further.

I turned the radio on and raised the volume, hoping that Marie would be able to hear her music when she woke.

That night, after we had eaten dinner and my mother had fixed soup for Marie, my father stood at the kitchen table and said, "Gail, maybe you and David would like to go for a walk. I want to speak to Marie again."

My mother began to stack dishes but my father stopped her. "Those can wait. I want to talk to Marie right now. While she's awake."

"She might want me here. She might feel more comfortable."

"Yes, she might, but I'm afraid Marie's comfort isn't what's important now. This is something that has to be done. You and David go outside."

Since he had questioned Marie before when I was in the house I figured that this time it was my mother he didn't want around. But she didn't seem to understand, and she persisted.

She said, "There might be some ways I can help."

By this time my father had retrieved a small notebook from the pocket of his suit coat. He stopped flipping its pages to say to my mother, "Did you hear me, Gail? Some of this I'd just as soon you didn't hear."

Was he being gallant—sparing his wife from hearing the particulars of his brother's alleged crimes? Or was he protecting his brother and keeping the number of witnesses to the accounts of his crimes to a minimum?

My mother and I didn't go far. That was all right. She wasn't much for taking walks and I was child enough to think I was too old to go for walks with my mother. We stayed in the backyard, though it was big enough that if we did nothing but walk up and down its length we could have gotten our exercise.

We stood in the middle of the yard while a gusty wind that lowered the temperature twenty degrees in less than an hour whipped my mother's hair in front of her face and wrapped her skirt tight against her legs. A cool front was moving through—sure to ruin the fishing, the local fishermen would say. My mother shivered and folded her arms. "I should have brought a sweater," she said.

"Do you want me to get you one?"

"*No,*" my mother said sharply. "No. You stay out of there. Your father's doing . . . official business."

I swallowed hard. I had already decided that I was going to ask my mother, once we were alone out there, why my father was talking to Marie. I knew the reason, of course, yet I wanted my knowledge out in the open. I wanted to be included, to know more than what my eavesdropping brought me. I supposed I wanted adult status, to have my parents discuss this case in front of me, not to have to leave rooms or to have people shut up when I came near, or worst of all, have them speak in code as if I were a baby who could be kept in ignorance by grown-ups spelling words in his presence.

Yet now that I had the opportunity, alone with my mother, my courage was running out. I wasn't sure which prospect was more unsettling: that she wouldn't tell me anything and would scold me for prying, or that she would reveal everything and I would have to hear that story coming from my mother's lips.

Finally I emboldened myself enough to ask a quick, awkward, suitably vague question: "What's going on, anyway?"

My mother kept her face turned to the wind but had closed her eyes against the blowing dust.

"Oh, there's some trouble going on with the Indians. Possible trouble, I should say." Now she was as cautious as my father.

"Why does he have to talk to Marie? When she's sick."

She took a long time in answering. Obviously her mind was elsewhere, somewhere off with the wind. "He thinks Marie might have some information."

"I thought the BIA handled Indian problems."

"He's just helping, dear. It's not so much."

"It's not so much" was a phrase my mother inherited from her mother. I had heard Grandma Anglund use it for occasions ranging from a scraped knee (mine) to a family burned out of its farm. It was her Norwegian way of keeping all our earthly

64

affairs from achieving too much importance.

My mother wandered a few steps away and stopped next to the one tree we had in our backyard, a towering, spreading oak exactly in the center of the lawn—precisely in the spot that kept the yard from being a boy's perfect football field.

"I love the wind," she said, tilting her head up to catch as much of it on her face as she could. "It reminds me of North Dakota. My goodness, how Dad used to curse the wind. 'Carrying away the topsoil,' he'd say. 'Giving it to South Dakota.' But I always loved it, that feel of rushing air. Bringing something new, was the way I felt."

"Makes good fishing," I said. "Riffles the water so the fish can't see you."

She turned a slow circle. "But the wind has a different smell here. In North Dakota it always smelled like dirt. Even in the middle of winter with all that snow there could still be the smell of dirt in the air. As if the wind came from some open place that never froze. But here the wind smells like the mountains. Like snow. Like stone. No matter how far away the mountains are, I still feel them out there. I can't get used to it. I never will. I guess I'm a flatlander at heart."

Had I any sensitivity at all I might have recognized that all this talk about wind and dirt and mountains and childhood was my mother's way of saying she wanted a few moments of purity, a temporary escape from the sordid drama that was playing itself out in her own house. But I was on the trail of something that would lead me out of childhood.

"Is Marie in trouble?" I asked. "Is Ronnie?"

"What? Oh, no. No, nothing like that. Your dad just wants

to see if she can give him some information. Answer some questions."

I looked back at the house. I could see, in the kitchen window, my father's form. I wondered how long he had been watching us. "He's out," I said. "We can go back in."

My mother turned and waved in my father's direction. If he saw he gave no sign, yet he remained in the window.

"The sun must be in his eyes," she said.

"Let's go in."

"You go ahead. I'm going to stay out here for awhile."

"And sniff the wind?"

She laughed. "Something like that."

The following Sunday the wind that my mother loved was still blowing as we drove out to my grandparents' ranch. We were traveling in our new Hudson that my father bought that year, and even that big, heavy boat rocked slightly in the wind once we were out in open country. It was a hot day, yet we had to keep the windows rolled up to keep the dust and grit from blowing into the car.

Marie felt a little better, so we thought it might be all right to leave her for the day. Besides, Daisy was right next door, and she would look in on Marie. Later in the afternoon Doris Looks Away, a friend of Marie's, was going to stop by the house.

Neither of my parents spoke as we rode, and the silence in the car was as oppressive as the heat. I knew why they weren't talking. My mother wanted to refuse the dinner invitation because Uncle Frank and his wife would be there. My parents tried to keep their quarrels from me, but that morning I had heard my father say, "For Christ's sake, Gail. They're my parents. What am I supposed to do—break off with them too?" "You don't have to curse," was my mother's only response. The next thing I knew, we were getting into the car. The excursion was all right with me. I hadn't been out to the ranch in a while, and I was eager to see my horse and to spend as much of the day riding as I could.

As soon as we turned off the highway and onto the rutted, washboard road that led to my grandparents', loose gravel and scoria began to clatter under the car. A thick cloud of red-tan dust rose behind us. Almost shouting, my father said, "I've been thinking. What would you two think of taking a few days later this month and going down to Yellowstone? Camp out. See the geysers."

"A real vacation," my mother said. "The mountains."

"Why not," my father said, as he held the jiggling steering wheel with both hands. "Why not us?"

It wasn't much of an exchange, but I knew what it meant: my parents were no longer fighting. I also knew we wouldn't go to Yellowstone. My father disliked conflict so much that he would frequently make a promise or a suggestion—like a family vacation—intended to make everyone feel better. Unfortunately, often he did not keep the promises.

When we pulled up in front of the ranch house, Uncle Frank's truck was already there. Covered with the day's dust, the Ford looked even older and more battered than usual.

"They're here," my mother said softly.

My grandparents' house was built of logs, but it was no cabin; in fact, there was nothing simple or unassuming about it. The house was huge—two stories, five bedrooms, a dining room bigger than some restaurants, a stone fireplace that two children could stand in. The ceilings were high and open-beamed. The interior walls were log as well. And the furnishings were equally rough-hewn and massive. Leather couches and armchairs. Trestle tables. Brass lamps. Sheepskin rugs on the floors and Indian blankets on the walls. Hanging in my grandfather's den were two gun cases, racks of antlers from deer, elk, bighorn sheep, and antelope, and a six-foot rattlesnake skin. One of the few times I heard my father say anything disparaging about his parents was in reference to their home. He once said, as we drove up to the house, "This place looks like every Easterner's idea of a dude ranch." (For a Montanan there was no greater insult than to have your name associated with the term "dude.") My mother, who disliked ostentation of any sort, was especially offended by the house's log construction—usually symbolic of simplicity and humility. (Her parents' house was a very modest two-story white farmhouse—neat, trim, pleasant, but revealing nothing of the occupants' prosperity.)

And I?—I loved that house! It was large enough that I could find complete privacy somewhere no matter how many others were in there. The adults might be downstairs playing whist while I crept around upstairs, toy gun in hand, searching from room to room for the men who robbed the Bentrock First National Bank.

When I slept over I was given a second-floor bedroom with wide, tall windows that faced north, and I sat at those windows and picked out the Big and Little Dippers, the only constellations I could identify. Or I imagined that the wide porch was the deck of a ship and the surrounding prairie the limitless sea.

Grandpa stood on the porch to greet us. He was dressed in his Sunday rich ranch owner best—white Western shirt and string tie, whipcord trousers, and the boots that were hand-made in Texas. He was alone, and while we got out of the car he watched us as impassively as he would strangers. He had his hands thrust in his back pockets, and his big belly stuck out like a stuffed sack of grain. His legs were spread wide, as if he were bracing himself. He wore his white hair longer than most men—over the tops of his ears, curling over his shirt collar, and with bushy sideburns almost to his jowls. As he stood there the wind lifted his hair and made his large head seem even larger.

It was the first time I had seen Grandpa Hayden since I heard about Uncle Frank, and when I saw him towering there like a thundercloud I thought, he won't let anything happen to his beloved son. He won't. But what if it's his *other* son who's trying to do something. . . .

"Can I go down to the stable?" I asked.

"You certainly may not," my mother said. "You come in first and greet your grandparents and find out how long until dinner."

My mother lifted a cake pan from the front seat. When he saw it, Grandpa Hayden said in his booming voice, "What have you got in there? Damn it, Enid said you didn't have to bring a thing."

"Hello, Julian," my mother said as she stepped onto the porch. "I thought you liked chocolate cake."

Grandfather took the pan from her. "Don't even take it in there. Hell, they don't have to know about it. I'll take care of it myself."

"What are you doing out here, Pop?" asked my father. "Acting as the official welcoming committee?"

"Came out here to fart. I had sausage for breakfast, and I'm not going to stay in the house any longer and squeeze 'em in. Can't do it."

My mother took the cake pan back and went into the house. She hated talk about bodily functions even more than she hated swearing. Both were specialties of my grandfather.

My father took up a position at the porch rail next to Grandfather. "That wind's something," my father said.

"If you don't like wind," Grandfather replied, "you don't like Montana. Because it blows here 360 days a year. Better get used to it."

That was another of my grandfather's specialties—turning casual remarks so they became opportunities for him to pass on his judgments or browbeating opinions. I was about to go when my father turned around, stared at the house, and asked softly, "Pop, where's Frank?"

"He's in there poking and twisting your mother's shoulders. Trying to figure out if she's got bursitis. Hell, I know she's got bursitis."

"Can I ask you something, Pop?"

I had my hand on the handle of the screen door while my father watched me, waiting for me to go in before he continued. I went in the house but stayed right by the door so I could hear what my father said.

"It's about Frank. . . ."

Yes, tell him, I thought. Tell Grandfather. Tell him, and he'll take care of everything. He'll grab Uncle Frank by the shoulders and shake him so hard his bones will clatter like castanets. He'll shake him up and shout in Frank's face that he'd better straighten up and fly right or there'll be hell to pay. And because it's Grandfather, that will be the end of it. Frank would never touch a woman like that again. *Tell him.*

My father cleared his throat. "About him and Gloria not having kids. . . . You've got to go easy on that, Pop. They want kids. They're trying."

"You know that, do you? Frank tell you that?"

"Not right out, but—"

"They sure as hell look healthy. Glo might be tiny but she's got enough tit for twins. What's the problem? He's a goddamn doctor. He ought to be able to figure it out."

"Pop. Listen to yourself."

My grandfather's boot heels thunked on the porch planks. "Your mother and I thought we'd have more to show than the one grandchild. Nothing against Davy. But Christ—just the one? From both of you?"

"You know what she went through with David. After that we decided—"

71

"—and white," Grandfather interrupted. "We want them white."

The silence was so sudden and complete I thought at first that they saw me and that was why they quit talking. But I didn't move; if I did they'd see me for sure.

My father said something I barely heard: "What do you mean by that?"

Grandfather laughed a deep, breathy *cuh-cuh-cuh* that sounded like half cough and half laugh. "Come on, Wesley. Come on, boy. You know Frank's always been partial to red meat. He couldn't have been any older than Davy when Bud caught him down in the stable with that little Indian girl. Bud said to me, 'Mr. Hayden, you better have a talk with that boy. He had that little squaw down on her hands and knees. He's been learnin' from watching the dogs and the horses and the bulls.' I wouldn't be surprised if there wasn't some young ones out on the reservation who look a lot like your brother."

One of them approached the screen door, and I quickly slipped away from my hiding post and into the living room. I picked up the first thing at hand—a cigarette lighter that looked like a derringer—and began to squeeze the trigger over and over, each time scraping the flint and throwing up a small, pungent flame. I tried to make my concentration on the lighter seem so total that no one would suspect me of eavesdropping.

It was my father coming through the door, and as he did he said over his shoulder to Grandfather, "I suspect you might be right on that." To me he said, "Put that down, David. It's not a toy."

72

It was the second time I had heard my grandfather say something about my uncle and Indian girls. . . .

Neither my father nor my uncle married women from Bentrock, or from Montana, for that matter. (That was probably another reason for people to resent the Haydens. I could imagine someone from town saying, "Weren't any of the local girls good enough for the Hayden boys?") My mother, as I mentioned, was from North Dakota, and Gloria was from Minnesota. My father met my mother while he was in law school, and Frank met Gloria while he was in medical school at the University of Minnesota. My parents were married soon after they met; Frank and Gloria, however, had an on-again, off-again romance for years.

They were finally married in Minneapolis, Gloria's hometown. This was during the war, and Frank was home on leave. The wedding took place right after Christmas, and it was a small, quiet affair, with only a few friends and family in attendance. Grandfather paid for all of us to travel by train to the wedding and to stay in a hotel in Minneapolis. It was the first time I was on a train and the first time I stayed in a hotel.

The night before the wedding my father, Grandfather, Uncle Frank, an old college friend of his, and two of Gloria's brothers went out together for Frank's bachelor party.

They didn't return to the hotel until quite late. I was already asleep, but I woke up when my father came in. He was drunk—which made another first for me. I had never seen my father take more than one drink. I lay quietly in bed while my mother helped my father undress. She also tried to keep him quiet, but it was no use; he was too drunk and too excited to keep his voice low.

"You should have seen it, Gail," he said. "By God, it was something. This Minneapolis big shot, this city boy, wouldn't let up. Kept saying to Pop, 'Mighty fine boots. Mighty fine. Just hope you're not tracking in any cow shit with those boots.' Wouldn't stop."

"Shhh. Watch your language. David can hear you."

"Just reporting. That's all. Just saying how it was. Finally Pop says, 'You don't let up, I'm going to stick one of these boots up your ass. Then I'm going to track *your* shit all over this bar.' "

"Oh, Wesley!"

He laughed. Giggled would be more accurate. "I've got to say what happened, don't I? This city fellow thinks he's heard enough. He plops his hat down on the bar, takes off his glasses and sets them down too. He starts for our table. But by the time he gets there Pop has pulled out that little .32 revolver of his. Chrome-plated so it's the shiniest thing in the place. Hell, I didn't know he had it with him. Anyway, he's got that gun right in the fella's face, and the guy goes white. He's just white as a sheet. Pop holds it there for a minute, and then he says, 'Out in Montana you wouldn't be worth dirtying a man's hands on. Or his boots. So we'd handle him this way. Nice and clean.' And he keeps holding the gun on him. I thought maybe I should say something, but Frank reaches over and puts his hand on my arm. Frank's laughing to beat the

74

band, so he must know something. Finally Pop says, 'Now you head on out of here and you better hope the snow covers your tracks because I'm going to finish this whiskey and then I'm coming after you.' By God, Gail, you should have seen that fella hightail it out of there! Left without his hat and glasses. And Pop just sits back down and finishes his whiskey. Doesn't say a word. Meanwhile Frank's laughing so hard he gets *me* going and then neither one of us can stop. People are leaving the bar right and left—probably afraid of these wild and woolly cowboys from Montana—and Frank and I are howling our heads off. Then when we leave we notice that Minneapolis hasn't even *got* any snow. And that sets Frank and me off all over again. Oh, Gail, I wish you could've been there. The Hayden boys all over again. The Hayden boys and their old man."

By that time, my mother had gotten him into bed and was covering him. "I don't think you'll find this so funny tomorrow morning. You're lucky you weren't all arrested."

"They couldn't arrest us—we *are* the law!" My father found that idea hilarious. He started laughing so hard he could barely breathe. Soon he was coughing and choking, and then he had to rush to the bathroom. The next thing I heard was my father vomiting. He was in there so long I fell asleep before he came out.

After the wedding the next day on the train going back to Montana, my grandfather offered a box of chocolates to my mother, Grandmother, and me. My father couldn't even look at them, a fact that my grandfather found amusing. My grandfather had a sweet tooth, and he insisted those were the best chocolates in the world, available only from a small confectionary in downtown Minneapolis.

Soon they were all talking about Frank and Gloria and the wedding, how nice the ceremony was, what a lovely woman Gloria was, how they hoped for a happy life for the two of them. Then Grandfather said, "Now he's got himself a good-looking white woman for a wife. That better keep him off the reservation."

No one said another word. Every one of us turned to the window as if there were actually something to look at besides wind-whipped, snow-covered prairies.

At dinner I sat between my grandmother and Aunt Gloria. My grandmother, a thin, nervous woman who seldom spoke when my grandfather was present, concentrated during the meal on cutting her ham into small perfect triangles before she ate them. Whenever she passed a dish to me she asked quietly, "Do you like this, David?" and her questions seemed so eager and pathetic that I said yes to everything. As a result, my plate was piled high with sweet potatoes and cooked carrots and sliced tomatoes and cottage cheese and kidney beans and corn bread and ham. And I had no appetite.

Aunt Gloria chattered throughout the meal. She talked about the weather and the price of milk. She talked about how, even though the war had been over for three years, she still felt funny about throwing out a tin can. She taught first grade, and she talked about how she was going to make little construction paper Indian headbands for all her students, with their names on the feathers. She talked about her little brother who was in college in Missoula and who told her how the ex-GI's pushed the professors around.

I loved Aunt Gloria—she was sweet and beautiful and good to me—yet that day I couldn't bear to look at her. How could she act normal, I wondered, when she was married to Uncle Frank? How could she not *know?*

Those were the cleanest thoughts I had. The ones I tried to suppress went something like this: Why would Uncle Frank want another woman when he had a wife like Gloria? And this line of thought was nudged along by my own desire. I thought Aunt Gloria was more than pretty. . . .

A year earlier I had stayed with Frank and Gloria when my parents were in Helena for a law-enforcement convention. I usually stayed home with Marie or with my grandparents at the ranch when my parents were out of town, but during that time Marie was doing something with her family and Grandmother was recovering from gall-bladder surgery.

While my parents were gone, I came down with a case of tonsilitis, as I frequently did as a child. Uncle Frank gave me a shot of penicillin, and Aunt Gloria took better care of me than my own mother. She made me chicken soup and Jell-O, she brought me comic books and ginger ale, and she never let more than an hour pass without checking on me.

She came in late one night to make sure I was covered. I kept my eyes closed and pretended to be asleep, but when she bent down to feel my forehead I could smell her perfume. The scent itself seemed warm as it closed in on me. She backed away and went to the window, and I opened one eye. She was wearing just the top of a pair of pajamas, and as she stood before the window just enough light came in from the street lamp to silhouette her breasts perfectly. I closed my eyes again, out of both shame and fear of being caught looking.

From the doorway came Uncle Frank's whisper. "Is he asleep?"

"Shhh," Aunt Gloria whispered back. "Yes." She tiptoed out of the room. In the hall Uncle Frank said aloud, "So this is what it's like to have kids. Damn."

Before long, I heard them through the wall in their own bedroom. Their bedsprings squeaked rhythmically; I thought I could her breathing—a sound spreading through the house as if it were more than sound, as if it were a presence, like perfume, like darkness itself. Later I heard them in the bathroom together. I couldn't make out anything they said, but that didn't matter. By then I was concentrating on only one thing: one more reason to envy Uncle Frank.

It was shame again that Sunday that kept me from looking at Aunt Gloria during our meal. And the day had one more similarity to that night. As Gloria leaned toward me to take a plate of tomatoes from Grandmother, I smelled my aunt's perfume again. But the lush sweet floral scent—so out of place in that rough-timbered room and among all those odors of food—did not excite me this time. This time it made me so sad I wanted to cry.

As soon as the meal was over, I asked if I could be excused to go riding. My parents gave me permission so quickly I wondered if they were planning to bring up the accusations against Uncle Frank as soon as I was out of the house. No, not in front of Grandmother. My father might have said something to Grandfather, but they would have gone to any extreme to keep that from Grandmother. It was often said that she was "nervous," a term that did not merely mean, as it does when it is applied to someone today, that she fidgeted, bit her nails, or worried too much (though she did all three); no, it meant that Grandmother had a condition that could strike her down at any time, as if a virus lived quietly in her but could suddenly run loose on a moment's notice if something upset her. Everyone knew the importance of shielding Grandmother from shocks of any kind.

Before I left the dining room, my grandfather stopped me. "Hold on there, David. Wait up a minute." He got up from the table and went into his den.

He came back in just a moment, and he was carrying a gun, a Hi-Standard automatic .22 target pistol and a box of cartridges.

"Goddamn coyotes," he said. "They're getting worse than ever. You see any out there, blast away."

Like almost every kid in Montana I had my own little arsenal—a .22 for plinking at prairie dogs and snakes; a .410-gauge shotgun for hunting pheasant, grouse, ducks, and geese; and a 30-30 for hunting deer. But in my case, all were single-shot. My father believed there was nothing worse than sloppy marksmanship and wasting ammunition. Having only one shot was a great incentive for learning to make that shot count. The theory was a good one, but it did not prove out in my case. I was never a very good shot but I was awfully quick at reloading.

Handguns were different, however. They were somehow not serious, not for bringing down game but for shooting as an activity in and of itself, and therefore slightly suspect.

I looked eagerly at my parents for their permission. My mother didn't care for guns of any kind but she had long ago seen the futility of trying to keep them out of the hands of a Montana boy. She simply shrugged. My father might have been troubled by my having both a pistol and a gun that could burn so much ammunition, but he only said, "Coyotes. Just coyotes."

I took the gun and shells from my grandfather and walked slowly out of the house, but once I was outside I ran to the stable. Within minutes I had saddled Nutty and was riding at a brisk trot out to some sagebrush hills and rimrock ravines where I often played. I didn't actually think I'd see any coyotes out there, but I'd be far enough from the ranch that I could fire off as many rounds as I wanted without anyone hearing.

I shot up that entire box of bullets. There was so much gunfire out there that afternoon that the ground glittered with my casings and Nutty became so accustomed to the shots that he grazed right through the barrage. After a while his ears didn't even twitch at the continual *pop-pop-pop*.

The .22 had very little recoil but after firing clip after clip, my hand and arm felt the effects. My hand tingled as if a low-level electrical current was passing through it, and my arm felt pleasantly loose and warm from the wrist to the shoulder.

I could have used all that ammunition to improve my marksmanship, aiming carefully at my targets and slowly squeezing off one shot at a time, but I didn't. Instead I tried to see how fast I could fire off a whole clip, shooting into the ground just to see the dirt fly. When I had a target (pinecones, branches, knotholes) I often fired at it from the hip or threw a hasty shot as I was whirling around. Most of the time I missed.

But once. I shot and killed a magpie.

He was teetering on a branch, his black feathers glistening like oil and his long tail wavering to steady him in the wind.

Less than forty yards away, I brought the .22 quickly up to shoulder height and snapped off a shot with no more care than pointing my finger.

The bird toppled from the branch, but in the instant of its fall it had enough life left—or perhaps it was only the wind—to open its wings and in so doing slow its descent.

To confirm my kill I walked over to where the magpie lay. Its half-open, glassy green eye was already beginning to dust over. This wasn't the first time I had killed something and it wouldn't be the last, and I felt the way I often did, that extraordinary mixture of power and sadness, exhilaration and fear. But there was something new.

I felt strangely calm, as if I had been in a state of high agitation but had now come down, my pulse returned to normal, my breathing slowed, my vision cleared. I needed that, I thought; I hadn't even known it but I needed to kill something. The events, the discoveries, the secrets of the past few days—Marie's illness, Uncle Frank's sins, the tension between my father and mother—had excited something in me that wasn't released until I shot a magpie out of a piñon pine.

I felt the way I did when I woke from an especially disturbing and powerful dream. Even as the dream's narrative escaped—like trying to hold water in your hand—its emotion stayed behind. Looking in the dead bird's eye, I realized that these strange, unthought-of connections—sex and death, lust and violence, desire and degradation—are there, there, deep in even a good heart's chambers.

With my boot heel I dug a shallow depression in the hard-baked dirt and nudged the magpie into it. I kicked some dirt over the bird, just enough to dull the sheen of its feathers.

I took a different route back to the ranch, riding slowly along a pine-covered ridge that looked down on McCormick Creek, a stream I sometimes fished. I was scouting for places where the water was high enough to give the trout pools to gather in.

Less than a mile from the ranch, where the creek widened and was bordered by an expanse of rocky, sandy beach, on the near side I saw two men. I pulled up Nutty and watched until I could see who it was. Uncle Frank and my father were standing on the riverbank, and they seemed to be arguing. I was too far away to hear what they said, but they were gesturing angrily at each other and speaking over the other's words.

It was strange. From that height I noticed something I had never noticed before. I noticed how the two men were brothers in posture and attitude. Two men in dress pants and white shirts, each bent forward slightly at the waist almost as if he were leaning into the wind. Each pointed at the other like a schoolteacher scolding a pupil. And when each was done talking he leaned back, squared his shoulders, and put his hands on his hips—exactly the way my father stood while he listened to one of my excuses for not cutting the grass or doing some chore.

I figured my father must have been confronting his brother over Marie's accusations, and I wanted to get closer so I could hear what they were saying. I dismounted and, as quietly as I could, began to weave my way down the hill. About halfway down the trees thinned, so I had to stop or be seen. I hid behind a thick pine.

I still couldn't hear them, but I wasn't sure if it was the distance or the fact that they had lowered their voices. Now they were barely speaking. Uncle Frank was backing away and muttering something. My father picked up a rock, wound up as if he were going to throw it as far as he could, then simply tossed it into the creek. I watched the splash to see if a trout rose to check it out as they sometimes will. Nothing. I wasn't surprised. You weren't likely to get a trout out in the middle of a shallow creek on a hot day.

Then Frank took a sudden step toward my father. Frank's arms were spread wide, beseechingly, yet his movement was so quick it seemed threatening.

I still had my grandfather's pistol, tucked inside the waistband of my jeans. I took it out, thumbed off the safety, and rested the gun against the stub of a branch. My view of Uncle

83

Frank was unobstructed, and I steadied the sights on his head, right in front of his ear.

The gun was unloaded, of course, but I wondered at that moment what might happen if it weren't. And my first question wasn't, could I pull the trigger; it was, could I, from that distance, with that weapon, under those conditions—the wind, the slope of the hill—hit my target. Only after I decided, probably not—an unfamiliar gun, its small caliber, my poor marksmanship—did I wonder what might happen if I killed my uncle. Would everyone's problems be solved? Would my father be relieved? Could I get away with it?

While these thoughts were gusting through my brain, my father and his brother had come closer to each other. The next thing I knew they were shaking hands. I put the gun back inside my waistband. My father and Uncle Frank walked off together, their broad shoulders almost touching.

We left for Bentrock after dark, and I took my customary place in the backseat, where I could lean back and watch the stars out the back window. The wind had died and the night was clear. My parents were silent in the front seat until we were halfway to town. Then my father said without prelude, "I talked to Frank."

"Wes!" My mother whispered sharply and looked in my direction. I didn't move.

"It's okay," my father replied. Whether he thought I was asleep or that he wasn't going to reveal anything, I wasn't sure.

My father went on. "I think the problem's been taken care of. Frank said he's going to cut it out."

"Oh, *Wes*-ley!" Her words came out in a moan, and I almost gave myself away by leaning forward to see if my mother was in pain.

"What?" my father replied, his confusion apparent and sincere. "What is it?"

"What about what's already been done? What about that, that . . . *damage?*"

"It can't be undone. That's passed. That's over and done."

My mother's voice became so low and tender it seemed better suited for an expression of love than what she actually said. "That's not the way it works. You know that. Sins— crimes—are not supposed to go unpunished."

Even then I knew what the irony of the conversation was: the secretary lecturing the lawyer, the law-enforcement officer, on justice.

My father was silent for such a long time I thought the conversation was over. At last he said, "He'll have to meet his punishment in the hereafter. I won't do anything to arrange it in this life."

When we arrived home Doris Looks Away was still there, and she and Marie were sitting in the living room drinking coffee. Marie was wrapped in a blanket, but she said she felt stronger. She still had a cough, but it was not as tight and wracking as it had been. My mother felt Marie's forehead and pronounced the fever still present, but obviously it had gone down. Her eyes had lost that unfocused, feverish gleam, and her cheeks no longer looked inflamed but merely ruddy.

Uncomfortable in our presence, Doris left almost immediately. Marie announced that she was going back to bed. Before she left the room she turned to me and asked, "Did you ride today, Davy?"

I nodded.

"Did you ride far?"

I nodded again.

"And did you see a coyote?"

How did she know I was given a pistol for hunting coyotes? "No," I said, "but I was looking."

"He's hard to see when you look for him."

Those were the last words Marie spoke to me. The next day, Monday, August 13, 1948, Marie Little Soldier was dead. My mother came home from work at 5:15 and found Marie lying dead in her bed. By the time I came home at 6:00 (I had spent the day fishing with Georgie Cahill), the hearse—a Buick station wagon from Undset's Funeral Parlor —was backing out of our driveway and carrying Marie's body away. Uncle Frank's pickup was parked in front of the house. On the courthouse lawn across the street stood a few onlookers, and Mr. and Mrs. Grindahl next door were on their porch, staring at our house as if it might burst into flames at any second. From somewhere on the block came the steady *ratcheta-ratcheta* of a lawn mower—someone who didn't know that for the moment all usual activity had ceased.

When I saw the car from Undset's, I did not run to our house in fear or curiosity. I didn't have to. I knew, I knew immediately what had happened. What's more, I could have walked right past our house, down the length of Green Avenue and right out of Bentrock. I could have kept going and never returned, out of my town, away from my family, away from my childhood. I could have kept going and taken with me the truth of what had happened in that house. No one else knew, and I could keep going until I found a place where I could bury that secret forever.

But I didn't. I walked slowly up the driveway and into the garage. I hung up my fishing pole and tackle box and the stringer of freshly caught perch and bluegills and went into the house.

Everyone was still in the kitchen. My father was on the telephone. "Yes, that's right," he was saying. "Could you please tell her that. That's right. She's at Undset's now." My mother sat at the table. She was slumped and staring at the floor, but she had one hand on the tabletop and her fingers were tapping rapidly. Those two actions—the body slumped and the fingers tapping—seemed so mismatched it was as if they belonged to separate bodies. Uncle Frank leaned over the table, filling out a form of some kind. His medical bag was on the table too, and seeing it there where we ate our meals I realized how large it was, how if its black mouth opened, it could swallow all the light in the room.

The door to Marie's room was partially open, and I saw

her bed. The blankets and sheets had been stripped, and the mattress was tilted up off the box springs and rested on its edge on the floor.

My mother saw me and reached out to me with one arm; the hand with the drumming fingers remained on the table as if her arm was paralyzed.

I stepped into my mother's embrace, and as I did she leaned her head against my torso in a way that made it clear I was the one offering comfort.

"It's Marie," she said. "She didn't make it, David."

My father hung up the phone, and I looked at him. "She's dead, David. That's what your mother means. Marie died this afternoon."

I smelled like fish. That's what I kept thinking. I smelled like fish, and that was the reason I didn't belong in this room. It was that and not the secret I held, the fearful knowledge. . . .

The back screen door slammed and Daisy McAuley burst into the kitchen. "My God! My God! What is going on here?"

My father repeated the words he spoke to me. "Marie's dead, Daisy. She died this afternoon."

"Oh, my Lord! Oh no! Why, I looked in on her yesterday afternoon. She was doing much better."

Uncle Frank finished his form and stood up so straight he seemed to be at attention. "This happens," he said to Daisy. "Pneumonia patients can have a sudden relapse, their lungs fill quickly. . . . Or the heart can fail from the strain of dealing with the disease. And there may have been a preexisting condition. We don't know. I see this much more often, however, in older patients."

88

I saw the document that Uncle Frank had been filling out. Across the top it said in bold letters "Mercer County Certificate of Death."

"I also have the feeling," Uncle Frank continued, "that she may not have been doing as well as she wanted us to believe. I think the Indian way is to deny illness, to try to push through in the face of it."

"Her fever was down, I know that," said my mother.

Uncle Frank shrugged. "A fever can fluctuate dramatically."

Daisy sunk down so hard onto a kitchen chair that it scraped a few inches across the linoleum. "That poor thing. That poor young thing."

"Pneumonia is still a serious disease," Uncle Frank said sternly. "Very serious. We mustn't lose sight of that."

My father stood by the refrigerator with his back to us. He ran his index finger up and down the woven basket that covered the motor on top of the refrigerator. "I couldn't reach any of Marie's family. No answer at home or at the step-father's bar." He turned around and I saw he had been crying. "I'm going to drive out there. They have to be notified as soon as possible. . . ."

"What about Ronnie?" my mother asked.

My father nodded. "I'll get in touch with him too. And Doris. But Marie's mother first. She has to be the first."

He moved toward the door, car keys in hand. "Do you need anything?" he asked my mother.

She shook her head. "Just hurry back."

"I won't take any longer than I have to."

This was my chance. I could ride along with my father and, when we were alone, tell him what I knew. But my mother still had her arm around me, and until she let go it didn't seem right to leave. Besides, he was going to face more grief, and this room held all I could handle. (I hadn't realized until that moment how large a part of my father's job this was. When someone's son rolled his pickup on a county highway, or someone's father shot himself climbing over a fence when he was deer hunting, or when some woman's husband dropped dead of a heart attack in a hotel down in Miles City, it was my father's duty to notify the family. Or when a drunk lay down on the tracks right in the path of a Great Northern freight train, it was my father's job to find out if he *had* any family. To this day I cannot hear that phrase—"pending notification of next of kin"—without thinking that someone out there, someone like my father, is toting around a basket of grief, looking for a doorstep to deposit it on. To think I once believed the hardest part of his job would be the dangerous criminals he might face.)

Right after my father left, Uncle Frank excused himself, saying he had to look in on Janie Cassidy, who had an unusually severe case of chicken pox. My mother did not get up to see him out.

Daisy reached out toward my mother and patted the back of my mother's hand. "You took good care of her," said Daisy. "That girl got the best care she could get right here in this house."

My mother released me and put her hand on top of

Daisy's. "I could have stayed home from work. I could have looked in on her earlier. . . ."

Daisy urgently placed her other hand on top of my mother's so it looked as though they were playing that baby's game of mounding hands, pulling the bottom one out and placing it on top. "You don't talk like that," Daisy told my mother. "You took good care of that girl. *Good* care."

Then Daisy must have seen something in my mother's eyes, because she turned to me and said, "David, are you hungry? You must be hungry. . . . Why don't you go over to our house and help yourself to pie. I've got a fresh blueberry pie on the kitchen table. You go get yourself some before Len eats it all."

I didn't move. The next time Daisy spoke it was not a suggestion but a command. "Go. And help yourself to ice cream. Have all you like."

Because Daisy kept the curtains drawn and windows closed to keep the heat of the day out, the McAuley house was dark and stuffy. The house always had a strange smell, as though Daisy had found some vegetable to boil that no one else knew about.

I stood over the pie, wondering how I could make myself eat a slice when I had no appetite.

From another room a voice called out, "Who's there?" It was Len.

91

I went into the living room, where Len sat in an over-stuffed chair, his long legs extended. In the room's dimness Daisy's white lace doilies on the sofa and chairs glowed white, as if they were hoarding all the available light.

On the table beside Len was a glass of whiskey. I recognized its brown color and smelled its smoky-sweet odor in the room. This was a bad sign. At one time Len had been a heavy drinker, given especially to week-long benders when he would plunge so deeply into a drunken gloom that it seemed unlikely he would ever climb out. In Bentrock Len McAuley was so well liked and respected that everyone was relieved when he quit drinking. I felt as bad seeing that glass of whiskey as I had when I'd first heard Marie cough.

He turned his gaze to me. It seemed, to my untrained eye, steady and clear. But it remained on me a little too long before he greeted me.

"David. Quite a commotion over at your place."

"Marie died." The words—and the fact they conveyed—popped out so easily they startled me.

Len nodded solemnly. "Yes. I believe I'm aware of that. Yes."

The room's heavy, dusky air seemed to insist on silence, and speaking was a struggle. "My dad's going out to talk to her family."

Len continued to nod. "Yes. Your father would do that. Yes."

I wanted to get away, but I couldn't think of anything to say that would serve as an exit line. And then it was hopeless. Len kicked their old horsehair hassock—the first sudden move he had made—and as it tumbled my way he said, "Sit down, David." I couldn't refuse.

Len stared at me for a long time, and though his gaze was steady there was something unfocused about it, as if an unseen dust in the room was clouding his vision.

He took a swallow of whiskey and that seemed to start his tongue. "You know, David, how I feel about your family."

"Yes, sir."

"I have this job. Deputy sheriff." He looked down at his shirt as though he expected to see his badge there. "Which I owe to your granddad and your dad. You know what your granddad said it means to be a peace officer in Montana? He said it means knowing when to look and when to look away. Took me a while to learn that." Len leaned forward and pointed a long, gnarled finger at me. "Your dad hasn't quite got the hang of it. Not just yet."

He slumped back in his chair and looked intently around the room at floor level as if he were watching for mice or insects. I had heard about drunks and their pink elephants and I wondered if he was hallucinating. I wanted more than ever to get away, but there was something tightly wound even in Len's casual posture—slumped shoulders and long legs extended—that made me think he was feigning repose and inattention, and as soon as I made a move to leave, his booted foot would suddenly trip me up or a long-fingered hand would pull me down.

He stopped looking around the room and fixed his eye on the carpet in front of his feet. "Long time ago I wanted to say something to your granddad. . . . I wanted to tell him, don't let those boys run wild. Just because we're out here, a thousand miles from nowhere, you think it doesn't matter. Out here, nothing but rimrock and sagebrush. You think no one's going to care. But those boys have to live in the world. Rein 'em in a little. Don't break them, but pull 'em back. But I didn't. Never said a word. Now look at them." He jerked his head up as if he actually saw my father and uncle in the room. "A lawyer and a doctor. College and the whole kit. Sheriff and a doctor. . . . Your granddad could tell me a thing or two. . . ."

For an instant something parted, as if the wind blew a curtain open and allowed a flash of sunlight into the room. Did Len know what I knew?

I leaned forward. "Did you see something, Len?"

He sat up straight and peered at me as if he weren't sure of my identity. "Did you?" he asked.

There it was, my opening! Now I could unburden myself, find someone else to carry this freight. Certainly Len could be trusted. But there was that glass of whiskey and its odor of sweet decay on his breath. . . . What if we *weren't* talking about the same thing?

I jumped to my feet. "I forgot the pie! I was supposed to get the pie!"

Len smiled wearily. "Look after your mother. This'll be a hard time for her."

Was Len in love with my mother? The thought never occurred to me until I wrote those words. But now I remember all the small chores and favors he did for her around our house—planing a sticking door or fixing a leaky faucet, bringing her the pheasants he shot or the fish he caught. The way he removed his hat when he came into our house and fiddled with it, creasing and denting the crown, running his finger around the sweatband. Well, why not. Why not say he loved her? Why not say his was one more heart broken in this sequence of events?

That night I thought I felt death in our house. Grandmother Hayden, a superstitious person, once told me about how, when she was a girl, her brother died and for days after, death lingered in the house. Her brother was trampled by a team of horses, and his blood-and-dirt-streaked body was laid on the kitchen table. From then until the day he was buried my grandmother said she could tell there was another presence in the house. It was nothing she could see, she said, but every time you entered a room it felt as though someone brushed by you as you went in. Every door seemed to require a bit more effort to open and close. There always seemed to be a sound—a whisper—on the edge of your hearing, something you couldn't quite make out.

As I had so often been advised by my parents, I never believed any of my grandmother's supernatural stories. Until the day Marie died. That night I lay in bed and couldn't breathe. The room felt close, full, as though someone else was getting the oxygen I needed.

I turned on the light and got slowly, cautiously, out of bed and opened my window wider. That brought no relief. The curtain stuck tight to the screen as if the wind was in the house blowing out.

Close to panic, I went to my parents' room. From the doorway I called softly, "Dad?"

In a voice so prompt and calm I wondered if he had really been asleep, my father answered, "What is it, David?"

"I thought I heard something."

"What is it you thought you heard?"

I peered into the darkened room. My father was still lying down.

"I don't know. Nothing, I guess."

The sheets rustled and my mother sat up. "Is something wrong?"

"I thought I heard something. Nothing. It wasn't anything."

"Come here, David," said my father.

As I approached the bed he sat up and swung his legs to the floor. He patted the bed beside him. "Sit down."

I sat down and my father rubbed my back, massaging the thin band of muscle on either side of my spine. "What's the trouble? Can't sleep?"

Just that little gentleness, that little thumb-rub below my neck, was all it took, and the words spilled out of me. "I saw something. . . ."

"Really?" His voice was steady and low. "I thought you said you heard something."

"I mean earlier. This afternoon."

"What did you see?"

"Uncle Frank. Uncle Frank was here."

"Of course he was. Your mother called him right away when she found Marie."

"No, I mean before. Earlier."

His hand stopped rubbing. "What time was that, David?"

"I'm not sure exactly."

"A guess. Take a guess, David."

"Around three."

My mother crawled quickly across the bed to the other side of me. "What are you saying, David?"

"Shh, Gail. Let David tell it."

I drew a deep breath and with its exhale let the secret out. "I was going fishing with Charley and Ben and we had just come from Ben's house and we were riding our bikes along the tracks. We were going out to Fuller's gravel pit. Then I had to go to the bathroom. I didn't want to go all the way back to our house to go, so I used Len and Daisy's outhouse." (In 1948 most, but not all, of the houses in Bentrock had indoor plumbing, yet many homeowners chose to keep their outhouses operational. They saved water, for one thing, and they were useful in case of emergency—if the pipes froze in the winter, for example.) "I told Charley and Ben to go on ahead and I'd catch up. While I was sitting there I saw someone cutting across our backyard. There's a knothole you can see out of. I was pretty sure it was Uncle Frank. Then I got out and watched him go down the tracks. He was going toward town. I'm pretty sure it was him."

"You're *pretty* sure, David?" my father asked abruptly. "What do you mean, you're pretty sure?"

"I mean I'm sure. I know it was."

"Did he have his bag with him?"

"I think so. Yeah. Yes, he had it."

"Was he in the house? Can you be sure? Did you see him come out of the house?"

Next to me, my mother had pulled together a tangled handful of sheets and bedspread and brought it toward her face.

"I just saw him coming from that direction."

"So you didn't actually see him come out of our house?"

"Oh, Wesley," my mother said in a sobbed half-plea, half-command. "Don't. You've heard enough. No more."

My father stood stiffly and limped toward the window. His bad leg always bothered him most when he first got up. "And you say this was around three o'clock?"

He had long since stopped being my father. He was now my interrogator, my cross-examiner. The sheriff. My uncle's brother.

"I think that's what time it was."

"Think, David. Think carefully. When did you last notice the time? Work from there."

"At Ben's. He had to watch his little brother and couldn't go until his mom came back. She was supposed to be back at two o'clock, but she was late. So maybe it was a little before three."

"Did anyone else see Frank? Charley or Ben?"

"No. They didn't wait for me."

My father looked at my mother. "And you got home when—at five?"

She got up from the bed and put on her robe. "I told you that before. I came right home at five."

My father muttered softly to himself. "He could have been

looking in on her. Checking on a patient. Doctors look in on their patients. . . . She was fine when he left her. . . . Fine. Used the back door because the front was usually locked. . . ."

My mother tried to interrupt him. "Wesley."

But my father's reverie continued. "On foot? Truck wasn't working. Truck was parked down the street at another patient's house. Gloria dropped him off."

"Stop, Wesley."

My father gently rapped his knuckles on the window. He stood like that for a long time, tapping the glass and staring out at the night.

My mother rested her hand on my shoulder, and I took advantage of that kindness to ask, "Is this bad?" I still couldn't reveal what I knew about Uncle Frank, but again I wanted my parents to let me in. I wanted to know that what I was doing was right and that I wasn't simply ratting on my uncle. But my mother didn't answer me. She patted my shoulder reassuringly, and it was my father who finally said, "Bad enough."

I pushed a little harder. "Does this mean——"

My father cut me off. "Does anyone else know? Are you sure no one else saw him? Did you tell anyone else?"

"I didn't tell anyone, but. . . ."

"But what, David?"

"Maybe Len saw him."

My father took a backward step as if he were trying to avoid a punch. "Len?"

I nodded.

"Oh, God. God*damn*. Len saw Frank."

"Maybe. . . ."

My mother asked me, "What makes you think Len saw, David?"

"He said. . . . I don't know. He was acting funny. I just think he might have."

"That tears it," said my father. "If Len saw Frank. . . ."

"It doesn't change anything," my mother said. "Not a thing."

"Oh really? Maybe. If Len knows, he'll keep his mouth shut if I ask him. Or if Dad asks him. But he'll know. There he'll be, day after day. With that look. I'm not going to live with that look."

My mother turned on the lamp beside the bed. In its sudden brightness the first thing I saw was my father's bad knee. He was wearing boxer shorts and a T-shirt, and his knee looked inflamed, swollen, scarred, and misshapen, as if his kneecap had been put back in the wrong spot. I saw my father limping every day but I seldom saw the reason. I realized the pain he must have been in constantly, and that pain seemed strangely to connect with the anguish he felt over his brother.

As if he were suddenly self-conscious in the light, my father put on his trousers.

"One more thing, David," my father said as he buckled his belt, the only bit of western regalia he wore—a hand-tooled ranger belt with a silver buckle and keeper. "Why didn't you say something before?"

"I don't know."

"Well, you can go back to bed. Now *you* can get some sleep." In his voice I thought I heard both jealousy and resentment.

Unfortunately, I couldn't sleep well either. Half-asleep and half-awake, I lay in bed and thought about Indians. In my daily life in Montana I saw Indians every day. There were Indian children in school, their mothers in the grocery store, their fathers at the filling station. Objects of the most patronizing and debilitating prejudice, the Indians in and around our community were nonetheless a largely passive and benign presence. Even the few who were not—Roy Single Feather, for example, who seemed intent on single-handedly perpetuating the stereotype of the drunken Indian and who, when drunk, walked down the middle of Main Street lecturing passersby, cars, and store windows on the necessity of giving one's life over to Jesus Christ—were regarded as more comedic or pathetic than dangerous.

But that night Marie's death and too many cowboy and Indian movies combined to bring me a strange half-dreaming, half-waking vision. . . .

To the east of Bentrock was a grassy butte called Circle Hill, the highest elevation around. It was treeless, easy to climb, and its summit provided a perfect view of town. That night I imagined all the Indians of our region, from town, ranches, or reservation, gathered on top of Circle Hill to do something about Marie's death. But in my vision, the Indians were not lined up in battle formation as they always were in the movies, that is, mounted on war ponies, streaked with war paint, bristling with feathers, and brandishing bows and arrows, lances, and tomahawks. Instead, just as I did in my daily life I saw them dressed in their jeans and cowboy boots, their cotton print dresses, or their flannel shirts. Instead of shouting war cries to the sky they were simply milling about, talking low, mourning Marie. Would they ever come down from Circle Hill, rampage the streets of Bentrock, looking for her killer, taking revenge wherever they could find it? My vision didn't extend that far, and finally I fell completely asleep, still watching Ollie Young Bear and Donna Whitman and George Crow Feather and Simon Many Snows and Verna Bull and Thomas Pelletier and Doris Looks Away and Sidney Bordeaux and Iris Trimble all walking the top of Circle Hill.

# Three

❀ ❀ ❀

WE had planned, of course, to attend Marie's funeral, but when my father asked Mrs. Little Soldier about when and where it would be, he was told that Marie would not be buried in Montana. Her family was coming from North Dakota and they would take Marie and her mother back to their home in North Dakota. When my father told my mother about this conversation, he said, "I tried to tell Mrs. Little Soldier that this was Marie's home also and that we thought of her as a member of the family, but she didn't want to hear. She wants to get out of Montana as quickly as possible."

My mother nodded knowingly. "Try to find out where we can send flowers. It's the least we can do. And we have to do something."

Quietly my father replied, "I am doing something, Gail. You know that."

I knew what he meant. In the days right after Marie's death my father was working all the time. He left early in the morning, and he did not return until late at night. When he was home, he was on the phone. (He left his office a few times to come home and use the telephone; there were some matters he didn't want to discuss in his office.)

His work habits were familiar enough to me that I knew

what was going on: he was building a case, and my father did this the same way he ran for reelection—by gathering in friends and favors. I suppose he was collecting evidence as well, but that part was never as obvious to me. What he seemed intent on doing—just as boys at play do, just as nations at war do—was getting people to be on his side.

Earlier in the year there had been a controversial arson case. Shelton's Hardware Store burned to the ground, and my father suspected Mr. Shelton, a well-liked businessman, of setting the fire himself to collect the insurance money. While my father conducted his investigation I was amazed at the change in him. I saw him on the street or in the Coffee Cup, telling jokes and laughing at the jokes of others. He passed out cigars like a new father. He inquired about families; he asked if there were favors he could do for people. Then, when he felt he had garnered enough good will, he made his arrest, exactly at the moment when his popularity was highest in the county. Naturally the consequent community feeling was, "Well, if Sheriff Hayden says it's so, it must be so." That feeling frequently carried juries as well. Mr. Shelton was convicted of arson and sent to Deer Lodge State Penitentiary for five years.

In short, rather than become grim and dogged when closing in on a suspect, my father became good-humored and gregarious. He became charming. He became more like his brother.

In the few days following Marie's death there was one significant change in this usual pattern. . . .

Three days after my mother found Marie dead in our home, around four o'clock on a rainy Thursday afternoon, my father brought Uncle Frank to our house. I had had something planned for the day with my friends, but the rain changed my plans, so I passed the day indoors, working on a balsa-wood model of a B-29 bomber. When my father and Uncle Frank came in the back door, I was at the kitchen table, my fingers sticky with glue and a hundred tiny airplane parts spread out on a newspaper in front of me. Uncle Frank walked in first, and he greeted me jauntily. "Good afternoon, Davy me boy. Wet enough for you?" He was carrying a small satchel, but it was not his medical bag.

He saw what I was doing and asked, "What's that you're working on?"

I showed him the box the model came in. "B-29."

"The B-29," he said. "I saw a few of those overhead. Always a welcome sight."

My father came in right behind Frank, and about him there was nothing of Frank's good cheer. Unsmiling and mute, my father simply pointed toward the basement stairs, and the two of them crossed the room and descended, my father closing the door behind them.

They were down there a long time, but I didn't move from the kitchen. I strained to hear what was going on in the basement, but I heard nothing. Finally, when slow, heavy steps began to climb the stairs, I pretended to be concentrating on my model, though I hadn't fitted a single piece since they came in.

My father came through the door—and he came through

alone. He closed the door tightly behind him.

He looked exhausted, as though climbing the stairs had taken all his energy. His face was pale, and he simply stood still for a moment, his back against the basement door. Then he went to the cupboard under the kitchen sink, rummaged around for a moment, and came out with a bottle of Old Grand-Dad. He took a juice glass from the shelf, poured it half full of whiskey, then held the glass to the rain-streaked window as if he were examining the liquid for impurities. He tilted his hat back on his forehead, raised the glass to his lips, closed his eyes, and took a small sip.

I watched him and discovered that adults could, like kids, be there yet not be there (as I often was in school). As my father took another drink of whiskey, this time a longer one that shuddered through him, I could tell that he was making a long journey while he stood in our kitchen. I waited until I thought he was back and then asked as softly as I could, "Dad?"

He put his finger to his lips. "In a minute, David. All right? Your mother will be home soon, and I only want to tell this once. We have a new development here."

So my father and I remained silent. He continued to sip his whiskey, and I packed up all the tiny pieces of my model plane. The rain clattered and gurgled through the gutters around the house. Once—only once—I thought I heard a noise from the basement that could have been Uncle Frank moving around.

But was that possible? How could Uncle Frank make any noise when my father had killed him?

I almost believed that.

I almost believed my father had taken his brother to a corner of the basement and—and what? Strangled him? Clubbed him? Shot him with a pistol equipped with a silencer? He had somehow killed him soundlessly. My father had tried to find a way to bring his brother to justice for his crimes, but finally, inevitably, unable to do that, he had opted instead for revenge. He had taken his brother into the basement and killed him. What else could explain that look on my father's face?

When my mother came home from work, she took one look at my father and asked, "Wes, what's wrong?"

He pointed to the basement door. "Frank's down there."

Both my mother and I stared at him, waiting for him to go on.

My father took off his hat and sailed it hard against the refrigerator. "He's in the *basement*. Goddamn it! Don't you get it—I've arrested him. He's down there now."

He stared at us as if there was something wrong with us for being more mystified than ever. Then he turned around, and instead of explaining to us he addressed the rain. "He didn't want to go to jail. Not here in town."

"Frank's in the *basement*?" my mother asked.

My father turned back to us but didn't speak. He walked over and picked up his hat. He looked it over and began to reshape it, denting it just so with the heel of his hand, pinching the crown, restoring the brim's roll with a loving brush-and-sweep. He dropped his hat in the center of the table and said solemnly to me, "My brother—your uncle—has run afoul of the law. I had to arrest him. You understand that, don't you? That I had no choice?"

He looked close to tears. "I understand," I said.

My mother had her purse open and was looking frantically through it as though she could find among its contents the solution to this problem. Without looking up from her search, she asked, "Where in the basement?"

"In the laundry room. I've locked that door." He held up the key for proof.

Our basement was unfinished, but the laundry room and its adjoining root cellar were closed off from the rest of the basement by a heavy wooden door (the door used to be in a rural schoolhouse; my father rescued it when the school was going to be torn down). The room where Uncle Frank was locked had a wringer washer, an old galvanized sink, the shower where I had once seen Marie naked, a toilet, and a couple of old dressers for storing blankets and winter clothes. The root cellar had wooden slats over a dirt floor, and shelves stacked deep with jars of home-canned pickles, tomatoes, rutabagas, applesauce, and plum and cherry jam. In another section of the laundry room was our ancient furnace, a huge, silver-bellied monster sprouting ductwork like an octopus's tentacles.

"In the basement?" repeated my mother.

"I wheeled the roll-away in there. He can sleep on that. I'll take him something to eat after we've had our supper."

"You've turned my laundry room into a *jail*!"

"Look," said my father, "Frank said he'd come with me

110

without a fuss. But he'd like to keep this quiet. He didn't want to be locked up in the jail. I said I'd respect that, and he's going to cooperate. Cooperate—hell, he's acting as if this is all some kind of joke."

"Who knows he's here? Have you talked to Mel?" She was referring to Mel Paddock, the Mercer County state attorney. If my uncle were formally charged with a crime, it would be up to Mr. Paddock to bring those charges on behalf of the state. Mr. Paddock and my father were good friends; during every election they pooled their resources and campaigned together for their respective offices.

"No one knows about this but the people in this house. I talked around it with Mel, but I didn't name any names. First I'm going over to tell Gloria." He looked at his watch. "I should go over there now. I figure she has a right to know—"

"—that you have her husband locked up in our basement." My mother groped for a chair as if she were blind. She sat down heavily and let her head rest on the heel of her hand.

"I'm not saying this is the best—"

My mother stopped him with her question. "How long?"

"I'm not sure," my father replied. "I'm going to call Helena in the morning. Talk to the attorney general's office and see if we can't get him arraigned in another county. Or maybe I'll check with Mel, see if we can do it quickly, get bond set—"

Again my mother interrupted him. "What are you going to tell Gloria?"

"Maybe that Frank's in some trouble. . . ."

"Tell her the truth. She's going to hear it anyway. Don't lie to her."

He nodded gravely but made no move to leave the kitchen.

"Go *now,* Wesley," urged my mother. "She has a right to know where her husband is."

My father took out his handkerchief and blew his nose—had he been crying quietly and I hadn't noticed? He put on his hat and went out the back door.

After a moment he was back, calling me outside. "David, could I see you out here?"

I went out immediately, thinking that now my father was going to tell me, man to man, what Uncle Frank's offense was.

The rain had almost stopped, and my father was waiting for me along the west side of the house. He stood back under the eaves and seemed to be examining the house's wood.

"Look here, David." He pointed to a section of siding. I looked but couldn't see anything.

"What?"

"The paint. See how it's blistered and peeling?" With his fingernail he flicked a small paint chip off the house. "It flakes right off."

I didn't understand—was there something I was supposed to have done?

"We're going to have to paint the house," he said. "But before we do, we're going to have to scrape it and sand it right down to bare wood. Then prime it good before we paint it. And we might have to put two coats on." He picked off another paint chip. "It's going to be hard work. Think you're up to it?"

"I think so."

He looked closely at me as if he were inspecting me for signs of peeling, chipping, or flaking. I must have passed inspection, because he clapped me on the shoulder and said, "I think so too. As soon as we get this business with your uncle straightened out, you and I are going to tackle this job." Was this another of his promises—like a trip to Yellowstone—to make me feel better? Was this the best he could do?

Then, as if it really were houses and paint that he wanted to talk about, he turned back to the wall. "Though if it was up to me, I'd probably just let it go. Let it go right down to bare wood. If I had my way, I'd let every house in town go. Let the sun bake 'em and the north wind freeze 'em until there isn't a house in town with a spot of paint on it. You'd see this town from a distance and it would look like nothing but firewood and gray stone. And maybe you'd keep right on moving because it looked like nothing was living here. Paint. Fresh paint. That's how you find life and civilization. Women come and they want fresh paint." He looked up at the eaves and gutters, judging perhaps how tall a ladder we'd need. Then he rapped sharply on the wall, three quick knocks to warn it that Wesley Hayden and his son were coming with scrapers, sandpaper, paintbrushes, and white paint, paint whiter than any bones bleaching out there on the Montana prairie.

"One more thing, David."

"Yes."

"If there's any trouble and I'm not here, you run for Len. Understand? Get Len."

"What kind of trouble?"

"Any kind. You'll know."

"Len's drinking again."

"You just get him. Drunk or sober. Understand?"

"Yes."

My father held out his hand to test if the rain was still falling. It came back dry. "No putting it off. I'll go talk to Gloria. Remember what I said."

"Wait," I said. "Does Len know?"

"He knows."

At about nine o'clock that night my grandparents came to our house. My father, mother, and I had been sitting in the living room, paging through the *Saturday Evening Post* or the *Mercer County Gazette*, listening to the radio, trying not to think about the fact that a relative was being held captive in our basement. When I think now of how calm we all looked, how natural and domestic this scene was, I find it more disturbing than if we had been crawling around on our hands and knees, howling like wild dogs. When the knock came on the front door, all three of us jumped.

"David," said my mother, "see who's here, please."

I opened the door and saw my grandparents dressed as though they had just come from church. My grandfather wore a double-breasted brown suit, white shirt, and tie. My grandmother's dress was such a pale yellow that I noticed how deeply tanned she was from working long hours in her garden.

She said hello to me, but my grandfather pushed right past me.

My father smiled widely when he saw his parents. "Well, look who's here. This is a nice surprise—"

Grandfather looked swiftly and suspiciously around the room. "Where's Frank?"

My father creased his newspaper and set it gently down on the table. "Gloria told you."

Grandfather took another step forward. "Where is he? Where have you got him? I want to see him."

My father simply shook his head. "I don't think that would be a good idea. Not at this point."

Meekly my grandmother said, "Gloria was concerned. She wanted us to make certain Frankie's all right."

The muscles of my father's jaw bounced rhythmically. "He's all right. I told Gloria that."

Without my having noticed her movement, my mother had come around behind me. She rested her hands on my shoulders.

"Bring him out here," Grandfather demanded. "Now. Right goddamn now."

My mother's voice rose and cracked as she asked, "Wouldn't you like to sit down? I have some coffee. . . ."

Grandmother smiled sympathetically at my mother. She nodded toward her husband. "He gets so upset."

"Wesley," repeated Grandfather. "Get your ass in gear and get your brother out here now."

I suddenly felt sorry for my father—not as he stood before me at that moment, but as a boy. What must it have been like to have a father capable of speaking to you like that?

"This isn't about family," my father said. "This is a legal matter."

"Bull*shit*. Then why have you got him locked up here and not over at the jail? This is your brother here. My *son!*"

I looked at my grandmother. Didn't she want to say that Frank was her son too?

My father replied, "I wanted to save Frank some embarrassment. I don't know how long that's going to be possible."

My grandfather began to dig furiously through his coat pockets, and I suddenly remembered the incident in Minneapolis when he pulled a gun on a stranger. Why was my father just standing there, his hands hanging defenselessly at his sides? Didn't he know that his father was going for a weapon?

"Dad!" I said.

My father turned to look at me. My mother squeezed my shoulders hard, and my grandmother pleaded, "Julian, the boy."

My grandfather was the only one who wasn't staring at me. He pulled out a cigar and ripped off the cellophane.

My mother whispered sharply in my ear, "Go on upstairs, David. Right away." She pushed me away from her.

I was glad to get away, and I ran upstairs. But I also wanted to hear how this confrontation would play out, so I hurried to the spare bedroom, the one right over the living room. In that room was a hot-air register in the floor that, when opened, let you hear what was being said in the room below. I crouched down by the register, slowly eased open the metal flap so it wouldn't rattle or squeak, and laid my ear against the grate.

"Sit down, Dad," my father was saying. "Please. Let's all sit down and talk about this calmly and reasonably. Please."

They must have agreed, because my father next said, "That's better. There. Gail, why don't you get us some of that coffee. And get Dad an ashtray. We don't want him to have to put his ashes in his pants cuff."

I could tell my father was trying desperately to put everyone in as good a mood as possible. His voice had risen just as it did when he tried to tell a joke. (He was terrible at it—he'd get the parts out of sequence and often mangle the punch line.) My grandfather was grumbling—it sounds, I know, like a trite thing to say about an older man, but in my grandfather's case it was literally true. When he wasn't talking he continued to make noise, a sound like a combination of throat-clearing and humming, as though he was keeping himself ready to talk, keeping the apparatus oiled and ready to go.

"Now," said my father. "Do you want to hear my side of it?"

That struck me as an odd phrase. I hadn't thought of my father as being against his brother, not in any personal way. I preferred to think of it as though the law had taken a curve in its course, and as a result these two brothers had ended up on opposite sides of the road.

"He's supposed to have beaten up some Indian," Grandfather said.

"What?" asked my father. "What are you saying?"

"That's what Gloria said. Something about assaulting a goddamn Indian. Since when do you get arrested in this part of the country for taking a poke at a man, red or white, that's what I—"

"Whoa!" my father interrupted. "Wait. What did Gloria say?"

My grandmother's faint, quavering voice answered him. "She said you arrested Frank for assaulting an Indian."

My father must have gotten up, because his voice grew louder and softer as if he were moving back and forth in the room. "Mom. Dad. I didn't arrest Frank for simple assault. I don't know what Gloria told you. This is for sexual assault. I arrested Frank for . . . for taking liberties with his patients. With his Indian patients."

"Oh, for Christ's sake!" Grandfather said. "What kind of bullshit is this?"

"There's cause. I've done some investigating, Dad."

"You—*investigating*?" In those two words I heard how little respect my grandfather had for my father and anything he did.

"I've even found some women who are willing to testify. And some others who aren't quite ready to talk. Yet. But I'm betting that once they see their friends come forward, they will too. There are a lot of them, Pop. A lot."

The living room fell so silent I checked to make sure the register hadn't flapped shut.

Then my mother spoke, in the accomodating, eager-to-please way that she used only with Grandfather and Grandmother Hayden: "We could hardly believe it ourselves."

Misinterpreting what my mother said, Grandmother quickly, hopefully, said, "A girl could be so easily mistaken. A trip to the doctor. The fear. The confusion. An Indian girl especially—"

"Please, Mom," said my father. "Not *a* girl. *Many*. There's something to this. Please. Don't make me say more."

"Go on," Grandfather said, "get on out of here. Let him say it to me."

My mother said, "Come on, Enid. Let's go out to the kitchen."

For a moment I thought of changing my station, of running to a different register so I could hear what my mother and grandmother would talk about, but since the conversation in the living room promised to be more revealing, I stayed put.

"Ever since the war," Grandfather began, "ever since Frank came home in a uniform and you stayed here, you've been jealous. I saw it. Your mother saw it. The whole goddamn town probably saw it. But I thought you'd have the good sense not to do anything. Now you pull a fucking stunt like this. I should've taken you aside and got you straightened out. If it meant whipping your ass I should've got you straightened out."

There was another long silence before my father said softly, "Is that what you think?"

"That fucking uniform. If I could've got you in one, maybe we wouldn't have this problem."

"Is that what you think." This time it was not a question.

"What the hell am I supposed to think? Screwing an Indian.

Or feeling her up or whatever. You don't lock up a man for that. You don't lock up your brother. A respected man. A war hero."

"Stop it, Dad. Just stop."

But I could tell Grandfather couldn't stop. He had his voice revved up—after all the grumbling, the motor caught and couldn't be shut off. "Is this why I gave you that goddamn badge? So you could arrest your own brother?"

"Don't try to tell me law. Don't."

"Some Indian thinks he put his hands where he shouldn't and you're pulling out your badge."

"It's not that. If it was only that. . . ." Here my father's voice faded. I couldn't tell if he was walking away or if he had come up against something he didn't want to talk about.

Grandfather continued to press. "Well, what is it? What the hell's so big you have to take an Indian's side and run your brother in?"

My father said something that I couldn't hear. Neither could Grandfather, because he said, "What? What are you saying? Goddamn, speak up!"

My father's single-word response boomed so loudly I pulled back from the register.

"Murder!" my father shouted. And a second time even louder: "*Murder!*"

What sounded like a gasp—it had to be Grandmother's, as she and my mother ran into the room at my father's shout—came rushing through the grate like a blast of hot air from the furnace. And then something occurred to me that made it difficult for me to put my ear back to the register.

On the other end of the house, in the basement, Uncle Frank might have been doing exactly what I was doing, listening to his family's voices boom through the ductwork and discuss his fate. And to hear the shouted word "murder," Uncle Frank wouldn't need the aid of the heating system.

I couldn't shake the image—my uncle Frank with his ear to the basement ventilator—and then it seemed to me that if I were to return to my listening post, Uncle Frank and I could be connected, two ears attached to the same sheet-metal system. And what if Frank should speak, should suddenly shout his innocence—his voice would travel the entire house unheard to arrive at my ear!

After a couple of moments I calmed down. The voices below were going on without me, like a furnace that doesn't care if anyone is there to feel its heat or not.

Grandmother was sobbing, a series of jerky breaths like hiccups.

Grandfather said, "My God, boy. Look at this. Look at what you've done to her."

My mother said, "Here. Let me."

"I'm sorry," said my father.

"Who the hell's dead anyway?"

"Marie."

"She was sick! She had pneumonia, for Christ's sake!"

"He didn't deny it, Pop. There's evidence—"

Grandmother's crying intensified, and I could tell she was having trouble breathing.

"Evidence? What kind of evidence? Go-to-court evidence or a wild hair-up-your-ass evidence?"

"That's for Mel Paddock to decide."

"You brought Mel in on this?"

"Not yet."

"My God. My God, boy. Stop this now. Stop this before I have to."

"This isn't for any of us to stop or start. This has to go its own way."

Not for any of us? I thought again of how I held my uncle in the sights of my pistol, of how I held, even tighter, the secret information that Uncle Frank had been in our house the afternoon Marie died.

"Oh, Wesley, Wesley," Grandmother said in that special tone that mothers use when pleading with their sons. Could my father withstand its power? I couldn't hear him make any response.

"Get up," said Grandfather in a calmer voice. "Let's go. We're not going to beg him."

There was a general rustling about, some footsteps, and I knew they were moving toward the front door and away from my hearing. I heard my mother's voice, but the only word I could make out was "please."

The front door closed, but I waited before going downstairs. I don't know what I was apprehensive about: my grandparents were gone, my uncle was locked in the basement, yet I had reached the point where I was afraid of being with my parents as well. There was so much unpredictable behavior going on that it seemed unwise to depend on anyone. For the moment it felt safer to remain alone on the bedroom floor, within earshot yet out of sight and reach.

What finally lifted me from the floor and moved me back down the stairs? It was trivial, yet it bore out what a boy I was when all this was going on. In the kitchen was chocolate cake. My father had stopped at Cox's Bakery the day before and bought a cake, and it was sitting on the counter. A murderer may have been locked up a floor below and the molecules of his victim's dying breath still floating in the air, yet these were not strong enough finally to stand up to my boy's hunger for chocolate cake.

As I approached the kitchen where my parents were, I heard my father say, "Help me with this, Gail," and a chair scraped across the linoleum. I thought he might be moving furniture or changing a light bulb and needed her help.

I was wrong.

I came into the kitchen and saw my mother sitting by the table. My father was on his knees before her, and his head was on her lap. She was rubbing the back of his neck in a way that was instantly recognizable to me: it was exactly the way she rubbed my neck when I had a headache. Overhead, insects flew frantic circles around the kitchen light.

Before I could speak my mother saw me and said so softly I wondered for an instant if my father was sleeping, "Hello, David."

My father lifted his head and I could tell by his red-rimmed eyes that he had been crying. But that was not what concerned me.

At that moment my father looked so *old* (he was only thir-ty-eight at the time), and I knew for the first time how this experience with his brother was ruining him physically. Was that the moment I realized my father would die someday? Perhaps. At any rate I knew that the puffiness around his eyes, the deepening creases of worry across his forehead and around his mouth, his pallor, his slow, stiffening gait were all signs that he was growing weaker. I also knew that to continue to stand up to Grandfather, my father needed all the strength he possessed. And perhaps that would still not be enough.

As if she could read my mind, my mother said, "Your father's just tired, David."

Using his good leg to brace himself, my father pushed himself to his feet. "We're all tired," he said. "Let's hit the hay."

I wasn't tired, and I didn't want to go to bed. I wanted my parents to tell me what happened when Grandfather and Grandmother were there. Though I knew exactly what was said, I wanted my parents to interpret it all for me. I wanted them to explain it so it wasn't as bad as the facts made it seem.

But since my father was embarrassed because I saw him on the floor, I had to go to bed. My mother gave me a sympathetic look but said nothing. I turned to go up to my room but my father stopped me.

"David."

"Yes."

"If Grandpa should come here when I'm not home, you're not to let him in, understand?"

"What should I say?"

"You don't have to say anything. Just don't answer the door. It'll be locked. Front and back both."

"What about Grandma?"

My father blinked and tilted his head back the way you do

when you're trying to keep tears from spilling over. "Not Grandma either."

"Not ever?"

"Not until I tell you different."

That night I cried for the first time since that whole sad, sordid, tragic set of events began. My tears, however, were not for Marie, whom I loved, or my uncle, whom I once idolized, or for my parents or grandparents or for my community or my life in it—all, all changed, I knew, by what had happened. But that night I cried myself to sleep because I believed that I would never see my horse, Nutty, again. I remembered the way he lowered and twisted his head when I approached, as if he were waiting for me to whisper something in his ear, that long ear whose touch reminded me of felt. I remembered how I used to rub my fingertips against the grain of the tight, short hair of his forehead and then smooth the hair back down again. I remembered how, when I first put my foot in the stirrup, he seemed to splay out his legs slightly, as if he were lowering himself and bracing for my mount. One of the great regrets of my childhood had always been that I couldn't live on the same grounds as my horse. Now the distance between us seemed too great for either Nutty or me to travel ever again.

The next day was hot and windy. My mother stayed home

from work, and though she said it was because she had a headache, I knew that was not the reason. She was staying home so I wouldn't have to be alone in the house with Uncle Frank. Early that morning my father took breakfast down to Frank and stayed down there about half an hour. When he came up he said to my mother, "I'm going to see what other arrangements we can make."

Around ten o'clock my mother sent me to the grocery store, and within a few minutes of walking out of the house that morning I noticed that a change had occurred.

I was a Hayden. I knew, from the time I was very young and without having been told, that that meant something in Bentrock. Because my grandfather was wealthy and powerful, because my father—like his father before him—enforced the law, because my uncle treated the sick and injured (and—am I wrong in mentioning?—because their wives were beautiful), people had an opinion about the Haydens. In their homes, in the cafes and bars and stores, they talked about us. When one of us passed on the street, there were sometimes whispers in our wake. They may not have liked us—perhaps Grandfather bought someone's foreclosed ranch cheap or let his cattle graze someone else's range, or perhaps he or my father sent someone's brother or cousin to the state penitentiary, or perhaps we were simply too prosperous for that luckless, hardscrabble region—but our name was no joke. We were as close as Mercer County came to aristocracy. I never consciously traded on the Hayden name, yet I knew it gave me a measure of respect that I didn't have to earn.

But as I walked down our tree-lined street that morning, I

imagined, behind every curtain or pulled shade, someone peering out and seeing a Hayden and thinking not of power, wealth, and the rule of law, but of perversion, scandal, family division, and decay. If the citizens of Bentrock didn't know yet that my father had arrested his own brother for sexually assaulting his patients and murdering Marie Little Soldier, they would know soon enough. Then being a Hayden would mean having an identity I didn't want but could do nothing to disown or deny.

By the time I got to Nash's Grocery Store, my shame over my family name was so great I didn't want to go in. I finally got my courage up by convincing myself that it was too early for all the details of our scandal to have made the rounds yet. Still, I picked up the items my mother wanted and left as quickly as I could.

On my way out I almost ran into Miss Schott, riding down the street on one of her big palominos. Miss Schott had been my second-grade teacher (everyone's second-grade teacher was probably more like it), and since she had retired from teaching she devoted herself full-time to what had been her hobby—breeding, raising, and showing blue-ribbon palominos that were as fine as any in Montana.

She was a strong, stout, cheerful woman who, now that she was no longer teaching, always dressed in boots, dungarees, a bandana-print shirt, and a sweat-stained short-brimmed cowboy hat that looked too small for her big head. She lived just outside town, and she rode one of her horses in every day to check her post office box or to run errands. No one in Bentrock was ever surprised to hear the heavy, slow *clop-clop*

127

of Miss Schott riding down one of the town's streets, or to see one of her tall, golden palominos tied up along the side of Nash's Grocery or in the alley behind the Hi-Line Hotel, or to smell the horse's steaming turds in any of the town's gutters.

It is commonplace to refer to the narrowness and intolerance of small-town life, but it seems to me just the opposite is true, at least of Bentrock, Montana, in 1948. The citizens of that community tolerated all kinds of behavior, from the eccentric to the unusual to the aberrant. From Miss Schott and her palominos to Mrs. Russell, who was a kleptomaniac (storekeepers kept track of what she stole and then once a week Mr. Russell, the president of the bank, went around and reimbursed them), to Arne Olsen, a farmer, who never (*never*) bathed and was proud of the fact, to Mr. Prentice, the band director at the high school who liked his boy students better than he liked his girl students, to old Henry Sandstrom, who shot mourning doves in his backyard, cooked them, and ate them. To my uncle Frank who molested his patients. How many other secrets had our town agreed to keep?

When Miss Schott saw me, she greeted me cheerily, "Good morning, David. Is the summer flying by for you too?"

I couldn't answer her.

I remembered that she had once been Uncle Frank's patient. I couldn't recall the reason or how I had even acquired this knowledge—another overheard conversation, perhaps—yet it was the one fact at the moment that pushed aside all others. I looked up at her astride her horse, and all I could think of was—*What did Uncle Frank do to you? Did he touch you there? There? What did he put inside you?*

128

And then Loretta Waterman, a pretty high-school girl whose father owned the drugstore, walked by, her moccasins scuffing the sidewalk, and she waved to me or Miss Schott or Miss Schott's horse, and I forgot about what Uncle Frank might have done to my former teacher and instead I wondered about Loretta, *Did you go to Uncle Frank? Did he make you take off all your clothes? Did he look at you there? And there?*

I began to feel at once dizzy and ashamed and sick because this time, with Loretta, the thought of how Uncle Frank may have abused her did not disgust and anger me as it had with Miss Schott, but stirred me sexually.

I didn't want to feel any of what I was feeling. I hugged my sack of groceries and ran home.

Once I was in the house, my mother said, "Look at you. All red in the face."

I jerked my head in the direction of the basement door. "How long is he going to be here?"

"Not long. You know your father's working on that."

"Then what?"

"Then what *what?*"

"What's going to happen after he leaves?"

My mother put her finger to her lips and whispered her reply. "I imagine there will be a trial."

"Grandpa will just get him off. He can get everybody to do what he wants."

She shrugged and went back to slicing cucumbers. "You might be right about that." As an afterthought, she added, "But not everybody."

"So what's it all for?"

129

"We're—your father is doing what's right."

"But we're the ones getting the shitty end of the stick."

Usually language like that would get me sent to my room. My mother didn't even look up from her knife's work. "You might be right about that too."

I was the first to notice the truck circling the house. From my bedroom window I saw it drive through the alley in back, along the railroad tracks. Four men were in it, two in the cab and two standing in back.

After it went by a second time, slowly, I ran downstairs to see it go by in front as well. I crouched below the living room window and peeked over the sill—I didn't want them to see me—and when it went by this time I recognized one of the men. Dale Paris, the foreman at my grandfather's ranch, was in the passenger seat, his bare arm crooked out the window, his cap pulled low. Dale Paris was the only cowboy I knew who never wore a hat but instead a red-and-black checked wool cap, earflaps tied up in summer and down in winter. I didn't know much about the man. He was simply a lean, silent presence on the ranch. My only contact with him had occurred when I came back from riding Nutty long and hard one day, and because I was in a hurry or lazy or both I simply unsaddled him and put him back in the stall. I was on my way out when Dale Paris stepped out of the shadows, grabbed my arm hard, and said, "Your horse needs wipin' down."

The other men in the truck were probably also employees of my grandfather. If that were so, it didn't take much reasoning to figure out why they were in town. They had come for Uncle Frank. How did they plan to get him? I didn't care to speculate that far.

My mother caught me peeking out the window. "What are you so interested in out there?"

I felt I should protect her, though from what I wasn't yet sure. "Nothing," I replied.

My answer didn't satisfy her, and she pushed the curtain aside in time to see the truck pass, close to the curb and driving so slowly you could hear the engine lug in low gear.

"Who was that?" she asked.

"I'm not sure."

She looked at me a long time as though she knew I had the answer. When I couldn't resist the power of her gaze any longer, I said, "I think they're from Grandpa's ranch. I saw them drive down the alley."

Without a word, my mother spun and went toward the kitchen, where she could look out the back window. Each of us at our respective posts—I in front and she in back—we kept careful watch on the circling truck. It drove around the house two more times before stopping in the alley. That was when my mother called me to the kitchen.

"Who are they?" she asked again. "You know. Tell me."

I looked out the window again even though I knew who she was talking about. The truck was parked along the railroad tracks, at the end of our yard, and straight out from the house.

The men who had been riding on the truck's bed had gotten down and were standing by the cab, talking to the man in the passenger seat.

"I think that's Dale Paris," I said.

"Who?"

"He works for Grandpa."

One of the men standing by the truck pointed toward the house, and the other man nodded. I knew what they were noticing. The people who owned the house before us had once planned to finish the basement and rent it out as an apartment. Toward that end they had built a rear entrance, steps going down to a door into the basement. These men must have figured, with Grandpa's help, that Frank was in the basement, and that rear door was the way they were going in after him.

The two men in the pickup got out. My mother clapped me on the shoulder. "Call your father," she said. She remained at the window, as if it was important that she not take her eyes off the four men.

I gave the operator the number of my father's office— two, two, three, two—and when Maxine, my father's secretary, answered, I asked for him.

"He's not here, honey," she said in her Louisiana drawl. Maxine Rogers and her husband came to Montana in the 1920s, in one of the first waves of oil-drilling exploration. After her husband's death, Maxine went to work for my grandfather, and she had been in the sheriff's office ever since. She was a short, wiry woman full of what I took to be Southern charm. She had a streak of snow-white hair running from her forehead to the top of her head that I always

132

associated—totally without reason—with her husband's death. He was struck by lightning on a butte west of town. Maxine wasn't anywhere near him when it happened.

"It's important," I said. "Do you know where he is?"

"Couldn't say for sure. Haven't seen him for an hour or so. You might try Mr. Paddock's office."

"How about Len? Is he there?"

"Haven't seen him all morning."

"If my dad comes in, please tell him to come over to the house."

I turned to ask my mother the number of the state attorney's office, but she was gone. The wind gusted, the curtains reached into the room, and when I looked out the window I saw four men crossing our lawn.

They walked abreast of each other but spaced out so that together they took up almost the entire width of the yard. Three of the men were dressed identically in straw cowboy hats, white T-shirts, blue jeans, and boots, so they looked like some strange uniformed team crossing the lawn in formation.

They came on slowly, looking about, as if they expected to be stopped at any time. I looked for weapons—rifles or shotguns or pistols—but saw none. Dale Paris, however, had an axe, and he carried it loosely at his side, the axe head swinging close to his leg.

Before I could turn or call out to my mother that the men were approaching, she came back into the room.

She was carrying my father's shotgun and a box of shells. She put the box on the kitchen table, opened it, and took out two shells.

"Dad's not in his office. Len either."

She turned the shotgun over, looking for something, holding it awkwardly across her forearms and wrists, trying to cradle it, to balance it. When she found what she was searching for, the loading chamber, she tried to push in a shell. When she couldn't get it in, I said, "You have to pump it open."

She pulled back on the pump—the quick, smooth, oily clatter of steel on steel—and put in the shells. She pushed back up on the pump and the gun was ready to fire.

"It'll hold five," I told her.

She gestured to the box. "I've got more."

The sight of my mother loading that shotgun was frightening—yes—but also oddly touching. She was so clumsy, so obviously unsuited for what she was doing that it reminded me of what she looked like when she once put on a baseball glove and tried to play catch with me. I wanted to rush over to her, to help her, to relieve her of the awful duty she had taken up.

"It's got a tremendous kick," I said. "If you fire it you really have to brace yourself." I took a step forward. "Why don't you let me—"

"Get out of here!" she snapped. "Go! Go over to the courthouse. Find your father. Find *someone!*"

Before I left I looked out the window once more. The four men were closer, but they had not reached the house. They had closed their rank and were now side by side. I could see Dale Paris's face clearly, sharp, intent, wind-bitten. One of the other cowboys laughed about something, and Dale Paris shut him up with a word and a scowl as quick and definite as a coyote's snarl.

My mother still stood a few paces back from the window, but she hefted the shotgun up, holding it right below her breast, and pointed it toward the window.

"The safety," I said and reached up close—close enough to embrace her—and clicked the safety off. "You're ready."

She didn't take her eyes off the backyard.

"I'll be right back."

"Just *go!* Out the front door."

I ran across the street, took the stone courthouse steps two at a time, pulled open the door—everything, the steepness of the stairs, the weight of the door, seemed to slow me down. I ran up another flight of stairs to the opaque glass door with the stenciled black letters "Mercer County State's Attorney." I pulled the door open with such force the glass rattled in its frame.

Flora Douglas, the secretary, was there, stacking reams of paper inside a cabinet. She was perhaps in her sixties, a round-faced, large-jawed woman whose severe look was made even harsher by her rimless spectacles and her steel-gray hair pulled tightly back in a bun. In truth, she was a kind, gentle woman—unmarried and childless—who had doted on me since she baby-sat me as an infant.

"Hello, David." Her gold-backed teeth glistened when she smiled.

"Is my dad here?"

"He was here earlier. About an hour ago."

"Do you know where he went?"

"I'm sorry, I don't."

"Is Mr. Paddock here?"

She shook her head and shrugged helplessly.

"If my dad comes back, will you tell him to come home right away?"

"I sure will."

I ran from the house, down the stairs, and toward the jail in the basement. As fast as I was moving it seemed agonizingly slow when I thought of Dale Paris and the other men in our yard.

Maxine was at the counter out front where people paid their parking tickets. She was counting manila envelopes and whispering numbers to herself so she wouldn't lose count.

"My dad back?" I panted.

She popped her Beeman's gum before answering. "Not yet, honey." She went back to her count.

"Could you call him on the radio please?"

"He's not in his car. I thought he was someplace in the building."

"Is Len here?"

"Still haven't seen him." She finished the stack, and when she looked up at me she must have seen something she hadn't noticed before. "My God, David. What is it? Has something happened? Is it your mom?"

I was already backing away. "Just tell him to come home. Please. Right away."

I was running back across the street when the shotgun boomed, and its blast was so loud, so wrongly out of place along that quiet, tree-lined, middle-class American street that

136

the air itself seemed instantly altered, turned foul, the stuff of rank, black chemical smoke and not the sweet, clean oxygen we daily breathed.

I was panting hard anyway, and when the shotgun fired, my heart jumped faster and I was suddenly breathless, the air blown so far out of me I couldn't get it back for a second and I wondered—but didn't really—have I been shot?

Yet I kept moving and when I burst through the front door I let the screen door slam behind me and to my distorted hearing—both sharpened and dulled by the shotgun blast—it sounded like another gunshot.

My mother had fired out the kitchen window but from a few paces back so that the buckshot had a chance to spread slightly and not only tear a ragged hole in the screen but to pull in the path of its explosion the kitchen curtain.

I knew from where she stood, from the angle of the shotgun's barrel, and from where the buckshot flew that she hadn't shot anybody. She had simply fired in warning or general panic or both.

She raised the shotgun, pumped another shell into the chamber—the ejected empty shell skittered across the linoleum—as if she were as practiced with that weapon as she was with her typewriter.

She stepped to the window and shouted, "You get away from there! Get away from the house—do you hear me!"

I came up behind her—did she even know I was there?—and I planned on wresting the shotgun from her. The thought of my mother shooting someone seemed the worst possibility the moment held. It was not that I preferred being overrun and beaten or killed by those men, but they were still *out there*. My mother was there in front of me, now trying clumsily to poke the shotgun barrel out through the hole in the screen, and I wanted to protect her not only from Dale Paris but from herself and the life she'd have to lead with someone's blood on her hands.

But before I could stop her I saw something outside that made it unnecessary.

Len McCauley was stepping through the hedge that divided our property from his. He was hatless, barefoot, and his dungarees were riding low on his hips. His shirt was untucked and unbuttoned, flapping open in the wind. Even at a glance and from a distance, I could see how rib-skinny and pale his torso was, but there were ropey strands of sinew along his arms. Then I saw something that made the issue of muscle irrelevant.

In his right hand, held close to his side against his thigh, Len carried a gun, a long-barreled revolver, probably a .44 or .45.

Once he was in our yard Len broke into a long-legged lope. When he was about thirty feet from our house he dropped to one knee, brought his pistol up to eye level, rested the barrel in the crook of one arm, and aimed in the direction of the four men, who must have been by the back door leading to our basement. He said something quick and sharp. It sounded like "right there."

Was Len drunk? I don't know why I thought that. His shooting position may have been faintly comical—nothing like the cowboys in the movies—but his aim and his eye looked rock-steady. Maybe it was simply the sight of that skinny bird-chested old man suddenly appearing in our backyard with a gun in his hand, ready to save us from marauders. And since there was nothing in the realm of logic or rational thought to explain his being there, the illogic of drunkenness seemed as ready as anything.

Len gestured with his gun, indicating that the men were to move away from the house.

As they came into view, walking slowly and watching Len closely, Len stood up. He kept his pistol aimed—right at Dale Paris's head, or so it looked. One of the men had his hands up. Len said something to them again, and though I couldn't hear what he said, all four men began to walk quickly back toward the truck.

Len turned toward the house and the window with the blown-out screen. "Okay in there?" he called.

"We're okay!" my mother shouted back. Then she was hurrying toward the door, still toting the shotgun. She banged open the screen door as if she couldn't wait to get outside. I followed her, wondering why we were leaving the house now that it was safe.

The sun was shining, an unremarkable fact except that I felt, standing on our lawn, as if I had just returned from a strange, hostile country where there was neither sunlight nor soft grass. At the end of the yard the black truck and its four riders sped off, sending up a spray of gravel and raising dust we could taste even from our distance.

My mother laid the shotgun down gently and ran to Len McAuley's side. Because you do not leave a shotgun lying in the grass, even hours after the dew has burned off, I picked up the gun. It smelled of gun oil and cordite.

"Oh, Len," she said and put her arms around him. He did not return her embrace, but he raised one arm to keep his gun hand free.

My mother noticed me and, still clinging to Len, reached out to me. "David," she said. I felt as though she were asking me to step over and become part of a new family consisting of Len our protector, my mother, and me. I remained in place, holding my father's shotgun.

At that moment, with those thoughts of betrayal and loyalty running through my brain, my father came around the side of the house. "What is it?" he asked. "What's going on? Maxine said. . . ."

My father was sweating, red-faced, and out of breath. With his bad leg, even walking fast exerted him. His hands were empty, and in our little armed enclave that made him seem out of place, almost naked.

Len took a step back, and my mother left his side to run to my father's arms.

When he had held her long enough to reassure both of them that everything would be all right, my father asked again, this time to Len: "What happened here?"

Len gestured toward the yard's end, where the truck had been parked. "Dale Paris. Mickey Krebs. Couple other men who work for your pa. They were here, looking to bust your brother loose, I suppose." He nodded at my mother. "She gave 'em a warning with a load of buckshot. Sent 'em packing."

My mother said, "If Len hadn't come. . . ."

"Any of them hurt?" asked my father.

Len shook his head.

"David," said my father. "Are you all right? I hear you were running all over trying to find me. What do you think about all this foolishness?"

"Where were you?" I asked.

"I was up in the third-floor court room. Sitting in there with Ollie Young Bear. He's been doing some work on this. Says he's found some women from the reservation, two anyway, who are willing to come forward and testify against Frank."

"Which charge?" asked Len.

"Assault. Sexual. That's the best we can do. Nothing's going to happen with Marie. No chance of an indictment there. That's long gone."

"You better move on it. Some sharp lawyer's going to raise hell about you keeping him locked up like this."

Since the moment this scandal had broken only a few days earlier, this was the most explicit anyone had been in my presence. My father actually said the word "sexual" in front of me!

My father nodded at Len. "It's moving ahead right now. We'll have him up for an arraignment later today or tomorrow."

Without taking his attention from Len, my father walked over to me and gently, wordlessly, took his shotgun from me.

Len looked down at his bare toes in the grass. "How about your pop? He's not going to stand for any of it. Today was just his first try. He'll come at you again."

"I'm going to see about heading that off."

141

As those two men coolly discussed their plans for prosecuting Uncle Frank and protecting our home, my mother gestured to me. "Let's go inside, David." Len and my father stayed behind, as I knew they would.

Back in the kitchen my mother fussed with the window screen, pulling and twisting a few of the loose wire strands as if the hole could somehow be mended the way a small tear in a sweater could be rewoven. She finally gave up and closed the inside window.

Moments later my father and Len came in. My father leaned his shotgun in the corner just as he did when he returned from hunting.

"From now on," he said, "if I can't be here, Len will be. He's not going to the office; he's going to stay right here. He'll keep an eye on things. And I'm calling Dad today. Tell him no more stunts like this. This is my family. My house."

As my father spoke, the words bouncing out of him like something falling from an overloaded truck, what struck me was that he seemed to be apologizing. For what? I wondered. For not being there when those men came? How could he have known? He was at work, where he was supposed to be. For being Frank Hayden's brother? Julian Hayden's son? Even then I knew we were not responsible for the circumstances of our birth or the sins of our fathers. For locking up Frank in our basement? For living in Montana? For not working as an attorney in Minneapolis?

Perhaps my mother also heard that apologetic tone in his voice, because she was looking at him queerly.

"No, Wes," she said. Her voice was strangely mild. "You

142

don't have to do any of that." She sat down slowly, carefully, as though she wasn't quite sure she could trust the chair to hold her weight. "You can simply open that door." She pointed to the basement door. "Go ahead. Let him go. That will take care of everything."

My father stared at her, waiting for her to say something more—to say she was joking or exaggerating to make a point. But when no other word was forthcoming, he said, "You don't mean that, Gail."

"Oh, yes I do. Yes. I most certainly do mean that. Let him go. Get him out of here. Then I won't have to walk around my own house thinking I hear him breathing down there. I won't have to worry about him breaking out—bursting into the kitchen like, like . . . like I don't know what. A crazy man! And I won't have to worry about strange men breaking *in* to break him *out*. I won't worry about my son, whether I should keep him close to me or as far from the house as possible. I won't wonder when men come threatening if David should pick up the gun to drive them away or if I should. But at least I know I can shoot the thing now. So, yes. I mean it. Let him go. Let him do whatever he wants to do to whomever he wants. I don't care anymore. I just want my house back. I want my family safe."

By the time my mother finished, tears were sliding down her face.

My father didn't speak for a long time, and when he did, it was to Len. "What do you think?"

Len looked embarrassed, as if he had intruded on a husband and wife's private quarrel. But since my father asked, there was no getting out. He sniffed and said, "She's right. Might as well let him go. Even on the lesser charge you're going to have a hell of a time getting a conviction. In this town. With your pop. With who's going to be testifying against him."

"At least the word will be out on him," said my father. "Maybe it will stop."

Len said, "I don't think you have to worry. He's got the message."

During this conversation two things struck me: first, that the man they were discussing (and whose crimes they kept alluding to but now did not specifically mention in deference to my supposed innocence) was not some outsider, some Kalispell cowboy or Billings tough who got in trouble up here in my father's jurisdiction, but was my uncle, a man who had only recently stopped lifting me and spinning me around in a dizzying whirl of affection and roughhouse play when he came to the house. He was *Uncle Frank,* who tried to teach me how to throw a curve ball, who gave me expensive gifts for my birthday and Christmas, who made bad jokes all through my grandmother's Thanksgiving and Easter dinners, who every year went up to Canada to buy the best fireworks for our Fourth of July celebration. Who was married to Aunt Gloria, beautiful Aunt Gloria. Who murdered my beloved Marie. And I couldn't make all those facts match the last one. Just as I couldn't get my mind to wrap itself around the knowledge that he was in our basement, and when I tried to think of that the floor beneath my feet suddenly seemed less solid, like those sewer grates you daringly walked over that gave a momentary glimpse of the dark, flowing depths always waiting below.

Len said, "Your pop's going to keep coming. You have to know that. It's not going to be safe around here. She's right to worry."

My father stared at the floor so intently it seemed as though he too was concentrating on his brother below.

"You've got an election coming up," continued Len. "You've got to think about how something like this is going to play with the voters. This county is going to get split three ways by this. Some will stand by you. Not many. There's the reservation. The Indians in town. Your pa. And he'll call in every marker he can. This county is going to get torn up over this. This will make Mercer County look like the Indian wars and the range wars combined. We'll be a long time coming back from this."

My father kept looking down. "Did my father talk to you, Len?"

"When?"

"Recently. The last day or so."

Len paused for a long time. "He talked to me."

"What did he want? What did he ask you to do?"

"You don't want to know that, Wes. Your pa's wild right now. He's not thinking right. He doesn't know what to do."

"Did he ask you to come over here, Len? Did he ask you to get Frank out yourself? Did he tell you how to do it?"

Len shook his head. "Don't ask me any more. Your pa talked to me. Let's leave it at that."

"And you turned him down. Or you wouldn't be standing here right now."

Len patted his head awkwardly as if he were checking to see if he had his hat on. "You're the sheriff. I'm the deputy."

I thought a saw a trace of a smile flicker across my father's lips. When he finally lifted his head he looked briefly at my mother, at Len, then settled his gaze on me.

I was still child enough to believe, as children do, that when adults were engaged in adult business children became invisible. That was why it was so unsettling to have my father staring at me. What did he want from me? Was he waiting for me to express an opinion——I was the only one in the room who hadn't. Didn't he know——I was a child and ineligible to vote? How dare he bring me in on this now——I wasn't even supposed to know the facts of the case!

Young people are supposed to be the impatient ones, but in most circumstances they can outwait their elders. The young are more practiced; time passes slower for them and they are constantly filling their hours, days, months, and years with waiting——for birthdays, for Christmas, for Father to return, for summer to arrive, for graduation, for the rain to stop, for the minister to stop talking, for girls to stop saying, "Not now, not yet; wait." No, when it comes to patience, even the enforced variety, the young are the real masters.

So it was easy to outwait my father. I simply put on my best blank face and kept its dim light beaming toward him. Soon he turned away and, without saying another word to any of us, crossed the room, opened the door to the basement, and descended the stairs.

When the thudding of his steps stopped, my mother calmly asked Len, "How do you think Frank did it?"

146

"Marie?"

She nodded.

"Wouldn't be hard, I suppose. A doctor. He's probably got the means right there in his bag. Pills. A shot of something or other. Maybe he put a pillow over her face. Weak as she was, it wouldn't have taken much."

Talk as brutal as this I would have thought would upset my mother, but she didn't flinch. Neither did she shoo me from the room so I would be spared this talk. She was too tired to care anymore. This was the day she had fired a gun in the direction of four men. From her own kitchen. There was no point in worrying about what children heard. There was no point in protecting them from words when evil and danger were so near at hand.

She said, "There should have been an autopsy."

Len shrugged. "Someone's got to ask for one. And someone's got to have a reason for asking."

"But at least we'd know."

"And then what? If you know something for sure, then you've got to act on that knowing. It's better this way. You know what you want Wes to do. It'll be a lot easier for him if he doesn't know too much."

"Yes," my mother replied, chastened.

It bothered me that Len and my mother could talk so easily, freely, almost intimately. That ease seemed to depend on my father's absence. He left the room, and they relaxed and talked about what was really on their minds.

Len went to the sink for a glass of water.

"I'm sorry," said my mother. "Would you like some

coffee? Or—I think we have something . . . stronger."

Len waved his hand. "Got to go. Daisy must be wondering what's going on."

"I'm surprised she didn't come over."

"That shotgun blast. That's what's keeping her away."

Len tapped the kitchen window right over the blown-out screen. "Might as well just put up the storm window. August. It's not that long until it's time anyway." He finished his water, drinking it all as if it was really thirst and not nerves that brought it to his lips.

He turned to me. "How about it, David. There's a project for you. Take that screen down and put up the storm window for your mother."

"Right now?" I asked.

"Not now, David," answered my mother.

"I better get moving," Len said again. On his way to the door he plucked his gun from the top of the refrigerator as casually as if he were picking up a garden tool. "Just holler if you need me." He glanced at the basement door. "I don't think you're going to have any more trouble. Not now."

He left, and my mother and I remained in the kitchen, waiting for my father and Uncle Frank to come up the stairs. Neither of us spoke, but the room's silence was not the usual kind. It felt stunned, still vibrating, the way the air feels in the silence immediately following a gunshot. And something else: I knew that all around us—in the houses up and down the block—human ears were tuned to our frequency, listening to our silence and wondering, was that a shotgun? Where did it come from? Did it come from the Haydens?

148

I didn't want to be there when Uncle Frank came up. What were we supposed to say to him? Did you miss your wife? How do you like our basement? Are you glad to be out? Yet I couldn't walk away. As long as my mother stayed, I felt I had to as well. I wasn't protecting her—I no longer had any illusions that I could play that role—but I stayed out of loyalty. I wasn't sure what our family had become in those troubled days, but I knew we had to stay close together. We had been under siege. We had to shore up the walls of the family as best we could.

Then the waiting was over. Footsteps thudded up the stairs, dull booms that could be mistaken, if one hadn't heard the real thing so recently, for a series of tiny shotgun blasts.

But two men did not come through the door. It was my father alone, sputtering as if he had come up from underwater. Before my mother could say anything, my father waved his hand in disgust.

"I'll move him over to the jail first thing in the morning," said my father.

My mother let her head drop forward.

"He's guilty as sin, Gail. He told me as much." My father struck himself on the thigh with his fist. "Goddamn it! What could I have been thinking of? Maybe a jury will cut him loose. I won't. *By God, I won't.*"

My mother got up from the table and began to work. She set the sugar bowl, the butter, and a loaf of bread on the table. She was on her way to the refrigerator when my father stopped her. "Did you hear me? This is the way it's got to be. I'm sorry."

She opened the refrigerator and peered inside. "I'm not arguing with you, Wesley."

"You don't think I wish it could be some other way?" my father asked belligerently. "He's my brother—we grew up together, sucked the same tit!"

She slammed the refrigerator. "Wesley—"

"I don't care. I tell you, if you could hear him talk. As if he had no more concern for what he did than if . . . if he had kicked a dog. No. He'd show more remorse over a dog."

"Marie?"

My father nodded grimly. "Don't ask how."

She pressed her hand over her mouth, to hold back a curse or because she was gagging on what my father told her. Or on what he wouldn't tell her and what her imagination filled in.

"Do you see?" asked my father. "I can't let him loose. Not and live with myself."

My parents' usual roles had neatly reversed themselves. My mother now represented practicality and expediency; my father stood for moral absolutism. Yet when I looked at my father his expression was so anguished that it didn't seem possible that he was arguing on principle.

"We understand, Wesley," my mother said gently, but I knew her words would do nothing to diminish his suffering.

"David," my mother said clearly and calmly, a different voice for a different world. "We don't have anything to eat. Why don't you run down to Butler's and get some of those frankfurters, and I'll boil them. That'll be quick."

She wanted me out of the house. That I knew. But she tried to soften that banishment with a little gift. The food I loved more than any other was the frankfurters from Butler's Butcher Shop. She gave me five dollars. "And when you go by Cox's, if you see one of those lemon cakes in the window, why don't you get one. Or anything else that looks good to you."

Before I left the house I turned back to look at my parents. They had not collapsed into each other's arms as I thought they might. They were simply standing in the kitchen. My father had his arms folded and stared blankly at the floor again. But my mother was looking at him, the expression in her eyes tender and loving and frightened, the same look she lowered on me when I was sick.

I suddenly felt a great distance between us, as if, at that moment, each of us stood on our own little square of flooring with open space surrounding us. Too far apart to jump to anyone else's island, we could only stare at each other the way my mother stared at my father.

That night the jars began to break.

I woke around 1:00 A.M., startled but unsure of what had roused me. Then I heard it, a distant *pop* and a faint clinking. I searched the dark, not because I thought the sound was in my room, but because I felt, in my sleepy groping, that activating any of my other senses might help my hearing.

There it was again—that ringing-tinkling—plainly glass breaking. But where? What was happening?

I got out of bed to look out my window but before I got

there I knew the noise wasn't coming from outside. No, this was in the house. It was coming from the basement! From Uncle Frank!

I ran to my parents' room. Their door was open and the light was on, so I had no reluctance about walking right in.

They weren't there. Their pillows still held the indentations of their heads, and the blanket and sheet formed an inverted V in the middle of the bed, suggesting that they had both thrown away the covers from their own side of the bed. I ran out of the room and to the head of the stairs.

I stood there waiting, listening.

Another faint shatter of glass.

Was it a window? Was Uncle Frank breaking one of the windows, hoping he could crawl out the high, narrow opening and escape through one of the window wells? Had my parents gone to stop him?

No, there was no possible way he could squeeze through one of those windows.

Another crash.

At the bottom of the stairs the darkness lost some of its thickness and strength—a light was on somewhere downstairs. Was it my parents? Uncle Frank? Someone come again to break him out, someone who broke our windows to get in?

I ran downstairs, hitting each step as hard and loud as I could, hoping to embolden myself as much as to frighten off whoever might be there.

My father and mother, in their pajamas, were sitting on the couch. They were not touching each other, and they looked frightened and tired, like children who have been awakened during the night for an emergency.

"Dad," I said, "I heard—"

"I know," he interrupted. "The canning jars."

"He's smashing them," my mother needlessly added.

"He's got into the root cellar," said my father. "He must be breaking every jar in there."

"All my jars of tomatoes and rutabagas. The pickles. The plum jelly. The applesauce. That corn relish you like so much."

Another jar popped below us, and now that I knew what the noise was from I could make some distinctions among the sounds. The higher-pitched pops were the small jelly jars— tightly packed and sealed tight with wax. The bass-note crashes were the large pickle jars, full of liquid and screwed tight with canning lids.

My mother pressed her fist to her face. "When I think of the work I did. And Marie did. And Daisy. . . ."

"I'm not going down there," my father explained to me. "That's just what he wants. No, let him get it out of his system. He'll run out of jars eventually."

Another one crashed.

"He's throwing them," said my mother. "I can tell. He's not just dropping them on the floor, he's *throwing* them as hard as he can."

My father patted her arm.

"Who's going to clean up that mess?" she asked.

"You can go back to bed, David," said my father. "I'm going to sit up until things calm down."

Another one. Was he spacing them at exact intervals?

"Get some sleep," my mother advised. "It's been such a long day."

My father stood and approached me. He put his hand on my shoulder. That gesture, along with an occasional back rub, was the only sign of physical affection he bestowed on me. My mother, on the other hand, still kissed and hugged me frequently. I knew and had known since I was very young that this difference between them had absolutely nothing to do with unequal qualities of love but only with their abilities to demonstrate it. Nevertheless, I wished at that moment that I could stay there, stay and feel the reassuring pressure of my father's hand upon my shoulder.

"One more night, David," my father said. "Just one more night and he'll be out of here. Things will be back to normal."

He was walking me toward the stairs, his hand no longer simply resting on my shoulder but gently pushing, giving me direction. "Sleep late," he said when we got to the stairs. "Sleep as late as you can, and when you wake up the worst of this will all be over."

But I didn't sleep late. I couldn't. I fell asleep listening for the crash of the jars and I woke the same way, straining to hear breaking glass.

Was it silence that finally woke me? At around six o'clock I came awake. The morning was overcast, dim, so there was no sunlight flooding my room. Birds do not sing at a gray sky with the same vigor as at a blue one, so their songs were not

154

shaking me awake. From the basement there was no sound of Uncle Frank shattering jars. What else could it have been but silence?

I got up quickly and quietly, crept past my parents' closed bedroom door, and went downstairs. I was so happy to have our house's stillness restored that I wanted to enjoy it.

But I was startled when I entered the kitchen. My father was already up (or hadn't he gone back to bed?), sitting at the kitchen table. He was wearing a sleeveless T-shirt and the trousers to his light gray suit. He was barefoot, but his heavy black brogans were under the table. There was a copy of *Argosy* next to him, but it was unopened. He jerked his head up when I came into the room.

"David. You're up early."

"I didn't know anyone else was awake."

"I'm waiting until I hear him stirring down there. Then I'm going to hustle him out and across the street."

"And put him in jail."

"And put him in jail. That's right."

Perhaps because he was tired and I could see it—his hair uncombed, his beard unshaven, his eyes ringed with dark circles, his shoulders slumped—I finally realized what this day meant to my father: This was the day he would put his only brother in jail. There would never be another day like it in his life.

I wanted to say something to indicate that I understood and sympathized. And I did sympathize. But understand? I could not; no one could. The best consolation I could manage was, "Not a very happy day, I guess."

He shrugged, a gesture full of resignation and fatigue. "David, I believe that in this world people must pay for their crimes. It doesn't matter who you are or who your relations are; if you do wrong, you pay. I believe that. I have to." He pushed himself up stiffly from the table. "But that doesn't mean the sun's going to shine."

He began to make coffee, trying to be as quiet as possible while he filled the percolator with water and carefully spooned in the grounds. "It's funny, the story I keep thinking about this morning. I don't know if I ever told it to you. Can't even remember how old I was at the time. Nine or ten maybe, and Frank twelve or thirteen. We'd already moved into town, and Dad was sheriff. Anyway. A friend of mine—could that have been Cordell Wettering? I believe so—and I were playing out by the golf course one fall day. Back then that course wasn't much. Still isn't. But then it was really sad. It had sand greens and barely a tree on it. Except on the seventh hole where the fairway runs right along that old slough.

"Cordell and I were on our way somewhere, or back from somewhere, and we cut through the slough. I guess things were dried out just enough or matted down from a few freezes, but we started finding golf balls in the brush, dozens of them. I don't know why that was such a big deal for us— neither of us had ever golfed in our lives—but you know how it is. We couldn't have been more excited if it was gold nuggets we found in that slough. When we came up out of there we were just dripping golf balls. Our pockets were stuffed and we were trying to carry more than we could hold.

"But when we climbed out, there were the Highdog boys,

three Blackfoot brothers who were widely known as bad customers. The oldest brother must have been about fourteen; the youngest, he was a skinny little runt about our age but mean as a snake when he was with his big brothers. Over the years every one of them was in and out of trouble with the law, but the little one got life in the state pen for carving up a cowboy with a broken bottle over in Havre.

"Anyway, the Highdog brothers said the golf balls we were carrying were theirs. Said that slough was part of the territory they watched over—those were the words they used—so anything we found was their property.

"Now, Cordell and I were plenty scared—we'd heard our share of stories about those brothers—but neither one of us wanted to give up our golf balls.

"We took off, running as fast as we could, dropping golf balls as we ran. Those golf balls helped us keep a lead on them. Every one we dropped, they stopped to pick up.

"But they were gaining on us, and just when it looked as though they were going to catch us—over by the clubhouse, such as it was—we ran into your uncle Frank.

"He and some of his friends were hanging out in the parking lot of the golf course. They were with an older boy, Charley McLaughlin, who was rolling cigarettes for Frank and the others.

"Cordell and I weren't dumb. We ran over to Frank and the others and told them the Highdog brothers were on our tails. That was all they needed to hear. This was an excuse to get those Indians who had bullied so many kids. Now it was the Highdogs turn to run—with my brother right after them.

"Well, they didn't catch them but that was all right. The important thing was, they saved our bacon.

"When Frank heard we almost got ourselves scalped over golf balls, he couldn't stop laughing. For years afterward, he'd tease me about that day. 'Look out!' he'd say. 'Here come the Highdogs! Hide your golf balls!' I didn't care. I was so grateful to him just for being there that day—I mean, I felt it was a kind of miracle. My brother. Being in the one place in the world I needed him most. . . ."

When he finished his story my father was staring out the same window through which my mother had fired the shotgun.

"Would they really have scalped you?" I asked.

"Oh, no. No. I don't mean that literally. They were bad business but not. . . . They'd have worked us over, though. That's sure. Funny. I found out years later that they had a reason for wanting those golf balls. They were selling them back to the golf course. Those Highdogs. . . . I mentioned the little one ended up in the pen? The oldest Highdog was killed when he lay down on the railroad tracks just outside town. Drunk, trying to walk home. I remember Dad coming home after investigating the accident. He said it was the worst he ever saw."

The coffee stopped percolating, and the silence that abruptly followed seemed to startle my father out of the past and back to the kitchen. "Well. Did I hear him stirring down there?"

"I didn't hear anything."

"No? Maybe not. I'll take some coffee down. That should get him going. We'll get an early start."

He poured two cups of coffee and then put both cups on saucers, an action of such delicacy and formality that I almost laughed.

He had a cup and saucer in each hand, so he asked, "Could you please open the door for me, David?"

The door or its frame was warped so I had to push hard to get it open. When it came unstuck I deliberately did not look down.

"Do you want me to close it behind you?"

"You can leave it open. We'll be up in a few minutes."

How much time passed before I heard my father's cry— thirty seconds? A minute?

Certainly no more than that. Yet what I heard signalled such a breach in our lives, a chasm permanently dividing what we were from what we could never be again, that it seems some commensurate unit of time should be involved. Ten years after my father descended the basement steps. . . .

From out of the cellar's musty darkness, up the creaking steps, through the cobwebbed joists and rough-planked flooring came my father's wail—"Oh, no! *Oh my God, no!*"

I ran down the stairs. It felt as it sometimes does in dreams, as if I were falling yet still able to control myself, hitting each step for just the instant it took to keep me from tumbling headlong down toward the concrete floor.

I slowed when I reached the bottom, as though suddenly the fear of what I was running toward overtook my concern for my father.

The aroma of coffee was still in the air. In fact, it felt as if I were following that smell.

Then I turned into the laundry room and another odor replaced it. All those broken jars—the sharp vinegary smell of the pickling juices, the dill weed, the sweet apples and plums, the rotting, damp-earth smell of rutabagas and tomatoes, and another odor, sweeter, heavier, fouler than the others.

My father was on the floor of the root cellar, and when I first saw the blood swirled like oil through the other liquids, I thought he had cut his bare feet on the broken glass that was everywhere.

But I thought that only for an instant, for the split second before I saw the blood's real source.

Uncle Frank lay on the floor, his head cradled against my father's chest. The gash across Uncle Frank's wrist had already started its useless healing: the edges of the wound had begun to dry and pucker; the blood, what was left in him, had begun to blacken and congeal. I could see only his right arm, but I knew the cut there was one of a matching set.

I must have made a sound—a little gasp that cracked against my larynx—because my father turned toward me. His features were contorted for a sob, but his eyes were tearless.

"Go wake your mother, David. *Tell her to call Len*. Get him down here *right away*."

I backed away quickly, glad to have a mission that would take me out of the basement. My father stopped me with one more command: "And David, don't let your mother come down here. *Don't let her!*"

Then my father's tears broke loose, one more briny fluid to mingle on the basement floor.

I didn't run up the stairs. I couldn't. But the reason is not what you might think. My legs worked fine. Oh, I was shaken. What I saw in the basement set my heart racing and soured my stomach but was not what slowed me down.

No, I took my time climbing the two flights to my mother because I needed time to compose myself, to make certain I could keep concealed my satisfaction over what had happened.

You see, I knew—I knew! I *knew!*—that Uncle Frank's suicide had solved all our problems.

My father would not have to march his brother across the street to jail.

There would be no trial, no pile of testimony for jurors to sift through, trying to separate the inevitable one-eighth, one-quarter, one-half truths from the whole truth. No pressure on anyone to come forward and bear witness, no reputations damaged, no one embarrassed, no one chastised. . . . The town would not have to choose sides over guilt or innocence.

Indian women could visit a doctor without fear of being assaulted, violated by a man who had taken a vow to do them no harm.

We would no longer have to worry that Grandfather would mount an attack of some kind on our home.

Certainly there would be sadness—Aunt Gloria was a widow, my father was suddenly, like me, an only child, Grandma's tears would fill a rain barrel—but this grief would pass. Once the mourning period passed, we would have our lives back, and if they would not be exactly what they had been earlier, they would be close enough for my satisfaction.

What more can I say? I was a child. I believed all these things to be true.

As I climbed the stairs, I felt something for my uncle in death that I hadn't felt for him in life. It was gratitude, yes, but it was something more. It was very close to love.

# Epilogue

❀ ❀ ❀

WE moved from Bentrock on a snowy day in early December 1948, a day, really, when we had no business traveling. It was bad enough in town, where snow covered the streets; out in the country nothing stopped the wind, so roads and highways could easily be drifted closed. But the car was packed, the moving van had left the day before with our furniture, we had said our good-byes to those who would hear them. Doors were locked; minds were made up.

They had been made up, in fact, for months. Since shortly after Uncle Frank's suicide, when my mother abruptly said to my father, "I cannot continue living here."

I knew she did not mean the house alone but Bentrock as well.

And I knew it was not the macabre discomfort of living in the same rooms where two people had recently died. That was not what made living there impossible for her. She had her religious beliefs to see her through that.

But she had no resources that enabled her to live with the lies concocted in the aftermath of Frank's death.

It was decided (my use of the passive voice is deliberate; I could never be exactly sure who was involved in the decision: my parents, certainly, but others were probably involved as well—my grandfather seems a good bet. Len? Gloria?) to explain Uncle Frank's death as an accident, to say that he had been helping my father build shelves in our basement, that he fell from a ladder, struck his head on the concrete floor, and died instantly. The only outsider to see Frank's body—and who could thus contradict this story—was Clarence Undset, owner of Undset's Funeral Home. What bribes were offered, what deals were struck to secure Mr. Undset's silence, I never knew, but everyone seemed confident that he would never reveal what he saw when he took Frank's body away: the gashes in Frank's wrists.

Similarly, it was decided not to reveal any of Frank's crimes. What purpose would it serve? He would never molest anyone again. The Indian women of Mercer County were safe from him. Besides, as my letter-of-the-law father said, Uncle Frank was never convicted of anything; there was no sense clouding the air with accusations.

As a consequence of these postmortem cover-ups, it was possible for Frank Hayden to be buried without scandal and to be eulogized in the usual blandly reverent way—decorated soldier, public servant, dedicated to healing, dutiful son, loving husband, still a youthful man, strong, vital. . . . Finally even the minister had to confess some bafflement over a life so rudely, inexplicably cut off. Who among us can begin to understand God's plans for any of us? Who indeed.

None of these precautions on behalf of Frank's reputation was enough however to restore harmony in the Hayden family. At the funeral, all of us—Grandpa and Grandma, Aunt Gloria, my father, mother, and I—sat together in the same pew (a surprisingly small group, considering the clan's power in the county), but neither my aunt nor my grandparents would speak to us. At the cemetery they made a point of standing on the opposite side of the grave from us. Even I understood the symbolism: Frank's death was an unbridgeable gulf between us. Although my parents seemed only hurt by this snubbing (they shuffled away from the cemetery and did not return with everyone else to the church for the meal in the church basement), it angered me. If there was any sense, any purpose at all in Uncle Frank's suicide, if he killed himself for any *reason,* it was so these people—his wife, his parents, his brother, his sister-in-law—could be reunited after his death. But there was the open grave, and not one of us would dream of leaping across it.

Therefore, when my mother made her pronouncement about living in Bentrock, my father understood exactly what she meant, and he simply nodded, as if he had known all along that was so but had been waiting for her to say the words. He didn't argue; he didn't say, "This is our home"; he didn't accuse; he didn't say, "You've never liked this town or this house, but it's my home." He agreed with my mother and began immediately to dismantle our lives in Bentrock.

He arranged, first of all, to withdraw from the upcoming election, citing as his reason "another job offer—an opportunity to practice law and put all that schooling to use." This was before he had lined up the possibility of a job with a law firm in Fargo, North Dakota. Len McAuley's name was substituted for my father's on the ticket. There was no doubt Len would be elected. He ran unopposed.

Next, our house was put up for sale, and my mother called her parents to tell them we would be staying with them on the farm while we looked for our own place.

My mother withdrew me from school and was given, in a manila envelope, my records to be conveyed to my next school.

My parents said their good-byes—to Len and Daisy, to the Hutchinsons. To Ollie Young Bear. The number of people seemed so small that it diminished my parents' years in Bentrock, as if their time there hadn't really amounted to much at all. I kept my own farewells to a minimum, and to ease the emotionalism (and perhaps to trick myself and make leaving easier), I told many of my friends that we would probably be moving back the following summer.

There we were, our car so loaded down it seemed ready to bottom out as my father backed out of the driveway. As we were about to pull away, I shouted, "Wait!", opened the back door, and jumped out of the car.

I ran to the house and clambered up a snowdrift to the living room window. I wanted one last look, to see what our house looked like without us in it. If my parents asked what I was looking for, I had already decided what I would answer. "Ghosts," I would say.

The frost on the window made it difficult to see in.

No, that wasn't it.

The emptiness inside made it difficult to see in. The blank

room had even less pattern than frosted glass. The bland gray carpeting, the once-white walls trying to turn yellow—snow should have been falling and drifting in *there*.

My parents, bless them, did not honk the horn or yell for me to get back in the car. They waited, and when I turned back to them and saw them through the screen of falling snow, I wondered again how it could have happened—how it could be that those two people who only wanted to do right, whose only error lay in trying to be loyal to both family and justice, were now dispossessed, the ones forced to leave Bentrock and build new lives. For a moment I felt like waving good-bye to them, signalling them to go, to move without me. It had nothing to do with wanting to stay in Montana; it had everything to do with wanting to stay away from those two hapless, forlorn people. What kind of life would it be, traveling in their company?

In fact, it was not a bad life at all. After spending the winter with my mother's parents on their farm, we moved the following spring to Fargo. There my father got a job with a small law office and within five years his name was listed as a partner with the firm: Line, Gustafson, and Hayden, Attorneys-at-Law. My mother got her wish: my father became a lawyer. He finally had a job to go with that briefcase she gave him.

For a while she tendered hopes that I would follow in my father's footsteps and pursue a career in law. "Wouldn't it be something," she once hopefully said to me when I was in my teens, "Hayden and Son, Law Partners?" "Wouldn't it be more appropriate," I answered, "for me to be elected sheriff of Mercer County, Montana, and carry on that Hayden tradition?" She never said another word about what I should do with my life. My remark was cruel, yet it was kinder than the truth: after what I observed as a child in Bentrock, I could never believe in the rule of law again. That my father could continue in his profession I attributed to his ability to segment parts of his life and keep one from intruding on another.

For myself, I eventually became a history teacher in a Rochester, Minnesota, high school. I did not—do not—believe in the purity and certainty of the study of history over law. Not at all. Quite the opposite. I find history endlessly amusing, knowing, as I do, that the record of any human community might omit stories of sexual abuse, murder, suicide. . . . Who knows—perhaps any region's most dramatic, most sensational stories were not played out in the public view but were confined to small, private places. A doctor's office, say. A white frame house on a quiet street. So no matter what the historical documents might say, I feel free to augment them with whatever lurid or comical fantasy my imagination might concoct. And know that the truth might not be far off. These musings, of course, are for my private enjoyment. For my students I keep a straight face and pretend that the text tells the truth, whole and unembellished.

Our only link with Montana was Grandma Hayden. She wrote to us regularly and even visited us a few times until she became too ill to travel.

As far as I know, she never spoke of the events of 1948, but she kept us up to date on some of those who played roles in the tragedy.

Aunt Gloria left Montana less than a year after we did. She moved to Spokane, where her sister lived, and Gloria eventually remarried.

Len McAuley was unable to complete his term in office. He had a stroke that left him partially paralyzed, and he had to turn the badge over to his deputy, Johnny Packwood, who had been in the military police. Thus, the Hayden-McAuley control of the Mercer County sheriff's office was broken.

Len lived on a number of years after his stroke, but ironically, less than a year after Len's cerebral hemorrhage my grandfather had one too. Which he did not survive. He was dead within three days.

Two strokes. I used to think, my interest in symbol and metaphor far surpassing my medical knowledge, that they died from keeping the secret about my uncle Frank. They held it in, the pressure built, like holding your breath, and something had to blow. In their case, the vessels in their brains. In my father's case, it was not only the secret he held in but also his bitterness. Which eventually turned into his cancer. Well, there I go, blaming an incident that happened over forty years ago for what was probably brought on by Len McAuley's whiskey, my grandfather's cigars, and my father's diet.

My happiest memory of Marie, the one that gradually separated itself from the general tangle of pleasant, warm moments, was from the autumn before she died.

Unhappy with my general lack of success at team sports, I decided I would do something about it. By sheer disciplined practice, through diligence, I would overcome my lack of natural ability and become good at something. Football was the sport I chose, and I further narrowed my choice of skills by concentrating on just one aspect of football. I would become an expert dropkicker. Drop-kicking, of course, has long since ceased to be a part of football, but in 1947 players dropkicked field goals; they dropped the ball, let it hit the ground for the briefest instant, then tried to boot it through the goal posts. That fall I spent hours in the backyard, trying to dropkick a football over a branch of our oak, then shagging the ball and kicking it back the other way, back and forth, back and forth. . . .

One afternoon when I was practicing after school, Ronnie Tall Bear burst out the back door of our house, Marie close behind him. Although Marie was obviously chasing him, they were both laughing.

Ronnie ran across our yard. When he came to my football, he fell on it, rolled with it through the leaves, and came up running, exactly as he no doubt had done with recovered fumbles countless times in football practices or in actual games.

When Ronnie picked up my football, Marie was able to gain some ground, but now he began to run like the football

172

star he once was, tucking the ball under one arm, faking, spinning, stopping, starting, shifting direction. Ronnie turned when he came to the railroad tracks and doubled back toward me. Once he got close enough, he lateraled the ball to me. Now Marie, tiring and slowing but still pursuing, was after *me*.

For the next half hour we chased up and down the yard, throwing the football back and forth, running after each other. It was a game, yet it had no object and no borders of space or time or regulation. It was totally free-form, but we still tried to use our skills—throwing accurate spirals, leaping to make catches, running as fast as we could in pursuit or escape. I felt that what we played, more accurately *how* we played, had its origin in Ronnie and Marie's Indian heritage, but I had no way of knowing that with any certainty. All I could be sure of was that I never had more fun playing ball, any kind of ball, in my life.

When we were too tired to play any longer, we went back to the house by way of the garage. There my mother kept a gallon of apple cider. Was it Marie's idea to uncap it? No matter. We passed the cider around, each of us drinking from the heavy jug, the cool, sweet cider the perfect answer to the question, how do you follow an afternoon of running around in the warm autumn sun?

I believe I remembered that incident so fondly not only because I was with Marie and Ronnie, both of whom I loved in my way, but also because I felt, for that brief span, as though I was part of a family, a family that accepted me for myself and not my blood or birthright.

My wife, Betsy, lived in seven cities before she graduated from high school. All of the communities were in Minnesota, Wisconsin, and northern Illinois, and during one summer vacation we drove to each town so she could photograph her childhood homes. (My wife also teaches, and this trip was exactly the sort of thing that teachers, with all that time and so little money, are likely to come up with for their summers.)

Since Betsy was immersed in all this nostalgia, it was natural for her to suggest that we drive to Montana to see *my* boyhood home. No, I told her, that was all right; I had no desire to go back. This she couldn't understand, and I finally gave in and told her why I—why no one in my immediate family—wanted to return to Bentrock. I told her about what happened in the summer of 1948.

The story stunned her, but it also fascinated her. She couldn't wait for the next meeting with my parents, so she could ask them about their memories of that summer.

I could have warned her off. I could have told her that in my family that is a subject never discussed. We all know what happened—we know it is there, in our shared past, we don't deny it, but we don't talk about it, as if keeping quiet is a matter of good manners. But I didn't tell my wife any of this. I suppose I wanted to see what would happen when someone else brought out into the open a topic that had never been discussed in any detail in my presence.

A few months later we were all together, gathered at my parents' house for Thanksgiving dinner. We had been seated

174

for only a few minutes when Betsy said, "David told me all about what happened when you lived in Montana. That sure was the Wild West, wasn't it?"

My father, at this time, had already had one cancer surgery, and he was not strong, but at Betsy's question he slammed his hand down on the table so hard the plates and silverware jumped.

"Don't blame Montana!" he said. "Don't ever blame Montana!"

He pushed himself away from the table, left the room, and never returned to the meal.

Later that night, after everyone was in bed, I came back down to the dining room. I sat in the chair where my father had sat and lightly put my hands on the table. For an instant I thought I felt the wood still vibrating from my father's blow.